level.15 - A Fleeting New Game Plus

Presented by
AO JYUMONJI

Illustration by
EIRI SHIRAI

"This is..."
Merry turned to look up
at the tower.
"The Forbidden Tower..."

The moon hung
in the sky above.
"It's red..."
The red moon.
Wait...
Was the moon red?

Submerge.
Submerge it.
My own presence.
My very existence.

Grimgar

of

Fantasy

and

Ash

GRIMGAR OF FANTASY AND ASH, LEVEL. 15

Copyright © 2019 Ao Jyumonji
Illustrations by Eiri Shirai

First published in Japan in 2019 by
OVERLAP Inc., Ltd., Tokyo.
English translation rights arranged with
OVERLAP Inc., Ltd., Tokyo.

Follow Seven Seas Entertainment online at
sevenseasentertainment.com.
Experience J-Novel Club books online at j-novel.club.

TRANSLATION: Sean McCann
J-NOVEL EDITOR: Emily Sorensen
COVER DESIGN: Kris Aubin
INTERIOR DESIGN: Clay Gardner
INTERIOR LAYOUT: George Panella
COPY EDITOR: Dayna Abel
LIGHT NOVEL EDITOR: E. M. Candon
PREPRESS TECHNICIAN: Rhiannon Rasmussen-Silverstein
PRODUCTION MANAGER: Lissa Pattillo
MANAGING EDITOR: Julie Davis
ASSOCIATE PUBLISHER: Adam Arnold
PUBLISHER: Jason DeAngelis

ISBN: 978-1-64827-554-8
Printed in Canada
First Printing: June 2021
10 9 8 7 6 5 4 3 2 1

Grimgar of Fantasy and Ash

level. 15 — A Fleeting New Game Plus

Presented by
AO JYUMONJI

Illustrated by
EIRI SHIRAI

Table of Contents

Grimgar
of
Fantasy and Ash

"Awaken."

H E OPENED HIS EYES, feeling like he'd heard someone's voice.

It was dark. Nighttime, maybe? But not pitch-black. There were lights. Looking up, he saw small candles affixed to the wall. Not just one, but many, spaced evenly, continuing as far as the eye could see.

Where was this place?

It was kind of hard to breathe. He touched the wall, and it was hard and rocky. Little wonder his back was sore. This was no wall. It was just bare rock. Maybe he was in a cave... A cave? Why would he be in a cave...?

He didn't know. He had absolutely no idea.

Those candles were pretty high up. He might just barely be able to reach one if he stood—you know, *high*. Moreover, they didn't give off enough light for him to really see his hands and feet.

He strained to listen. What was this he was hearing? It was faint. People breathing, maybe?

"Is anyone there?"

There was a response.

"Uh...yeah."

"Yes..."

"Where is this place?"

"Nyaa..."

More than just one.

"Erm, I...I'm here."

"Wh-wh-what, wha... What's going on here? Someone help me..."

"I've gotta be hungover or somethin'. I feel like shit..."

"Would you stay away from me? You stink."

How many were there in total? Not just two or three. There were more. Men and women.

"Hold on..." He decided to take his chances. "Where...are we? Does...anybody know?"

The big guy nearby shook his head. "Nah..."

Had his eyes adapted to the darkness? He could see a lot better now.

"I...dunno," the big guy said. "I mean... Um, I'm... Uhh... What was it again...?"

"Huh... What?"

"I'm probably...Kuzaku."

"Ohh. Your name?"

"Yeah, but...I don't remember. I can't recall."

"Recall what? Ah!" He clutched at his chest, as if trying to claw something off it. He couldn't recall. He couldn't *remember*. Was this what the big guy was talking about?

"I'm the same..." he said at last. "Haruhiro... That's my name, but that's all I know."

How long had he been here? What was he doing in this place? Haruhiro was asking these things about himself. There was no reason he shouldn't know the answers. He thought hard, trying to recall.

Something tugged at the back of his mind. Suddenly, whatever it was vanished.

There was no way he shouldn't remember these things. Despite that, Haruhiro was at a complete loss. "What is this...?"

"Whoa, hold up," a woman spoke. "You don't remember?" She sounded highly dubious. "How far? How far back do you not remember?"

"How far back? What do you mean?" Haruhiro groaned as he tried to answer the question. His head felt heavy. There was a dull throbbing deep inside it. A weird pain.

Were there even pain receptors in the brain? There weren't, were there? In that case, did that mean this pain was fake?

As he sat there, unable to answer the woman's question, the big guy spoke. "No, I already told you," he said, "I don't know anything but my name."

"No way..." The woman was speechless.

"Yeah, weird, isn't it? I think so, too..." The big guy sniffled, then cocked his head to the side as he groaned in thought.

"The point is, we can't recall."

"You too, Haru? Not just Kuzaku?"

When the woman called him "Haru," he reflexively replied, "Yeah." It didn't immediately seem weird to him. The sense that something was off came after a brief delay. It was almost as if *she* knew who he was. That was the way she spoke to him, at least.

"Um, would you happen...to know me?" Haruhiro asked. "Maybe?"

"Know you? It's more than that. I—"

"Eek!" That scream didn't come from the woman to whom he was speaking, but from another one.

Haruhiro's eyes shot over to her. She was looking down, wrapping her arms around her own body. Haruhiro hurriedly looked away. The woman wasn't wearing any clothes. She was bare naked for some reason.

"Whoa, awesome!" Kuzaku stared intently at the woman, but then he covered his eyes and looked away. "Nah, I shouldn't."

It seemed Kuzaku hadn't ogled her deliberately but had ended up doing so because it was inevitable. "S-sorry! I'm seriously sorry!" He gave her a wholehearted apology.

It would be best if they could give her something to wear. As Haruhiro debated whether he should take off some of his clothes and offer them to her, someone threw the woman a dark-colored cloak.

"There ya go, wear that."

"Th-thank you..."

Once the woman put the cloak on, she seemed to regain

some measure of composure. Why had she been nude? From the way she was acting, she hadn't gotten naked of her own volition. Though it had been an unfortunate accident, this place wasn't bright enough for Haruhiro to have seen much of anything. He considered telling her that, but it was possible that would be negligible consolation at best, so he decided against it.

"For now, why don't we try and sort out what we know?" he said instead.

How many people were here? How many of them only knew their own names, and how many of them had memories? They couldn't even get started until they figured that much out. Or maybe they could; Haruhiro didn't know, but this information might give them some clue. Hopefully. He hoped so.

"I'm Haruhiro," he said. "I know I'm repeating myself, but I only know my own name."

"Ohhh. I'm Kuzaku. I'm the same as Haruhiro, I guess."

"Shihoru... Me too... I only know my name. Why was I naked...?"

"Setora. That's all I can recall as well."

"I'm Io, and other than that... Yeah, I don't know either."

"Gomi. That's all I know. I've got a name that literally means trash? Aw, come on..."

"Tasukete... It's scary that that's all I remember. Is that even a name? Tasukete. Or am I just crying out for help...?"

"IIIII'm Hiyo. That's all I can say for now, I guess?"

"Nyaa."

Mixed in with them was an animal that clearly wasn't human.

It looked similar to a cat, but it wasn't. The creature seemed used to humans. Or it was attached to Setora, at least.

"The little guy's all over you," Kuzaku said.

Just so, the creature wouldn't move away from Setora. "I wouldn't say I find that particularly disagreeable..." Setora cocked her head to the side. She didn't seem to know why, but she was petting the animal like a pro.

Setting aside the animal, which no doubt did not understand human speech, eight of them only knew their own names: Haruhiro, Kuzaku, Shihoru, Setora, Io, Gomi, Tasukete, and Hiyo. There was just one exception.

"I am...Merry." She was the only one who remembered more than her name.

It was eight-to-one, so people who only knew their own name were in the overwhelming majority. Maybe that was just how things were. Merry was the exception, and people generally went through life not knowing anything but their own name.

No, obviously not. This was clearly an abnormal situation. Even without his memories, Haruhiro could tell that much.

Merry pointed to Haruhiro, Kuzaku, Shihoru, and Setora in turn. "I know you. We were comrades."

In addition, she explained that the animal was what was called a "nyaa," and that Setora had been keeping him, as might have been expected. His name was apparently Kiichi.

"What about me?" Io asked.

"You," Merry answered, "were pretty well-known, so I'd heard rumors."

"I was well-known. Famous enough that people had heard of me..." Io covered her mouth with both hands. Was she surprised? She looked like she was trying to stifle a smile too. Was she pleased? Did that fact make her happy?

"Whaddaya know about me?"

"A-a-and me?"

According to Merry, Gomi and Tasukete were Io's comrades. However, she didn't know them and had just heard their names.

"My comrades?" Io shook her head repeatedly in disbelief. "These two, of all people?"

"I'm sorry..." Tasukete said, his voice becoming very small. He might well have been crying.

"Real nice way of saying it..." Gomi muttered to himself, but he seemed less angry and more crushed.

Incidentally, Io and her group weren't completely unrelated to Haruhiro and the others. There were apparently these large groups called "clans," and both of their groups belonged to the same clan. But because they'd never met directly, they had very little sense of camaraderie or fellowship.

According to Merry, she had been working together with Haruhiro, Kuzaku, Shihoru, Setora, and Kiichi as comrades. They had wandered into an unfamiliar place, gotten into a lot of trouble, and unfortunately been separated.

"That's as far as I remember. I'm sure a lot happened after that, though."

And the next thing she knew, here she was.

"I see," Haruhiro mumbled. He immediately questioned the

utterance. What, exactly, did he see? None of this made any sense. With no memories, he had no standard by which to make sense of anything, so there was no way he could be satisfied with the explanation.

Despite that, Kuzaku seemed to buy it completely. "Comrades, huh? Comrades. We're comrades." Kuzaku repeatedly nodded to himself. "Now that you say it, I get the feeling we are. It feels right to me, you know?"

It does? Really? Uhh, how? Haruhiro would have liked to interrogate him on that point, but it was true that he hadn't felt all that surprised when Merry revealed they were comrades. Though it might just have been that he couldn't *be* surprised. Still, he wasn't simply going to accept it and think, *Oh, okay. We were comrades, huh? I guess that means we're comrades now.*

"So, what about Hiyo?" Hiyo asked.

"You're..." Merry started to say something, then shook her head. "I don't know. Not me."

"Awww. Hiyo's the only one you don't knooow? Isn't that kiiiinda unfair?"

"I don't know that it's a matter of it being fair or not..." Haruhiro interjected despite himself.

"But, buuuut... It's no faaaair. No fair at all. Hiyo's the only one who doesn't know anything. But hold on, is just sitting here forever gonna do us any good? Hmmm?"

"That's, uh..." If you were to ask Haruhiro, *"Do you want to stay here forever?"* he would have had to say, *"No, not really."*

They seemed to be in a tunnel-like cave. He had no reason

to think this, but he felt like if they followed the candles, they'd find something.

"Well, let's go, then."

As Haruhiro tried to get going, Io stopped him. "Hold it. Why are you acting like you're in charge? Are you trying to make me do as you say?"

"I wasn't trying anything. Why don't you decide, then?"

"Oh, if I must." Io let out a deliberate-sounding sigh. "If you insist, I'll make the decision."

Haruhiro didn't really insist, but if he pointed that out, they'd probably end up squabbling over it. "So, what are we going to do?"

"Let's go."

So we're going, after all. Haruhiro only thought that. He didn't say it. Io seemed like a pain in the butt to deal with, and he wanted as little conflict as possible. That's why he stayed sitting, trying to give off an air of *Okay, would you please go now?*

But what was this? Io showed no sign of moving. After all that, she pestered Haruhiro. "What are you doing?" she said.

"What do you mean, what?" Haruhiro was dazed for a moment. "Huh?"

"Hurry up and go," Io said, gesturing in the direction of the candles with her chin.

It took another moment for that to register with Haruhiro. "Me?"

"Yes, you," Io continued. "It could be dangerous, right? Someone has to take the risk, but it's not going to be me. You agree, don't you?"

Io grinned. If he looked closely—no, even without looking that closely— Haruhiro could tell that anyone would agree that Io was beautiful and had a charming smile, but he could sense her intent to weaponize those two facts. Or was that too far-fetched?

But Haruhiro had been trying to take the lead to begin with. He could just look at this as things having gone all the way back around to where they started. Besides, somehow it felt natural to take point. It was just a vague sense he had. But it was strange at the same time, considering he also got the feeling that he wasn't an outgoing, social, or proactive kind of person.

"Honestly, none of this makes sense..."

When Haruhiro started walking, Kuzaku chased after him. Merry, Shihoru, Setora, and Kiichi followed while Io, Gomi, Tasukete, and Hiyo trailed behind them.

There was no telling how far the line of candles went. It was a bizarre situation. Yet Haruhiro wasn't that fazed. Had he lost his sense of reality? Or was he just unflappable to begin with?

Though on that note, the rest of the group didn't particularly complain or seem that uneasy either. Even when they saw what looked like an iron grate up ahead, everyone remained calm and no one panicked.

"Is that an exit?"

The iron grate looked like it could be opened and closed like a door. No—not *like* a door. It *was* a door.

Once they opened the door, they stepped into an unlit, narrow corridor. It stretched onward, reeking of mold. Haruhiro and the group continued down the corridor single file. He knew this wasn't a dead end. There were stairs at the end of the hall, and light shone down from above.

Huh? Haruhiro thought, and he almost stopped walking. He didn't stop, though. Suddenly, he got the sense he had been here before. But it was just a vague sense, not like his memories were returning.

When he climbed the stairs, there was another iron-grated door there. Beyond it lay a room made of stone. Haruhiro put his hand on the door, which was slightly ajar. He pushed it lightly, and it opened further with a creak.

Stairs led upward from that room. He didn't see a table, or chairs, or any other kind of furniture, but shelves lined the walls, and there were two lit lamps.

Speaking of the wall, what was that blackish handle-like thing sticking out of it? Was it for hanging tools of some sort? It might also have been a lever for operating something. Haruhiro investigated it closely, being careful not to touch it. No one told him to; he found himself doing so without even deciding to.

When he looked over, Tasukete was checking the shelves and tapping on the wall. His eyes met Tasukete's. An eerie light shone in the eyes Haruhiro glimpsed through Tasukete's awfully long bangs. It felt kind of awkward. Haruhiro looked away.

"Tasukete-san's a thief too?" Merry suddenly said.

"Ohh." Kuzaku clapped his hands, then cocked his head to the side. "Thief? Like a burglar? And 'too'? So Haruhiro's a thief too? Huh? Is he a robber?"

"No, that's not it..."

According to Merry, Haruhiro and the rest were volunteer soldiers for some country called Arabakia. But there were different kinds of volunteer soldiers. Since they were called "volunteer" soldiers, were there different types of troops or something?

Thieves were one type. They did reconnaissance, opened locked doors, and searched for dangerous traps. They weren't actually burglars, but they made use of a similar skill set and served a support role in combat.

"So I was a thief. Volunteer soldiers..." It was hard for Haruhiro to believe he had been a volunteer soldier—or any kind of soldier at all.

But when Haruhiro thought about it, he *did* have two short, knife-like blades hanging at his waist. Kuzaku and Gomi had much larger swords, and they wore what looked like armor too. From an objective perspective, Haruhiro and the others made for a dangerous-looking group.

Kuzaku was what they called a paladin, while Shihoru was a mage, and Merry was a priest. Io was apparently a priest too. Setora, meanwhile, was not a volunteer soldier at all, but a comrade who had joined them along the way.

Merry didn't know what Gomi and Tasukete were. In her estimation, Gomi was a warrior, or perhaps a dread knight. Tasukete was probably a thief like Haruhiro.

Haruhiro got the sense that being a thief suited him better than being a warrior or a mage. Tasukete wasn't super tall like Kuzaku, or like Gomi with his strangely grim face and stocky build. If anything, he was closer to Haruhiro.

Io glanced at Hiyo. "And her?"

"Hmm!" Hiyo pointed to herself. "You mean Hiyo?"

Merry gave Hiyo a sideways glance. "As for her—"

It seemed like there might be some hidden meaning in the way she looked at Hiyo.

"As for her," Merry began again, "Whether she's a volunteer soldier or not is...hard for me to say."

Hiyo chuckled. "Hiyo's not so sure about that, eiiiither."

Was she just joking around? Or perhaps she was trying to dodge the issue, judging by the way Merry was acting like something was up.

If Haruhiro thought about it again, weren't Hiyo's hairstyle—with her hair tied off to both sides—and her impractically over-decorated outfit kind of out of place?

"By the way," Hiyo said, pointing to the stairs that led up. "It looks like we can go up there. Now, what are we going to doooo?"

Grimgar
of
Fantasy and Ash

| **The Nightmare Continues**

HARUHIRO decided to climb the stairs with Tasukete. Everyone else would wait in the lower room. He got the sense it would be easier that way.

When he took one of the lamps off the shelves and climbed the stairs, he found another room. It also had a number of shelves, all of them packed with assorted things. There were wooden boxes and barrels stuffed between the shelves, as well as large jars.

A sizable table sat in the middle of the room. Several barrels placed around it looked like they would have worked just right as chairs. There was an unlit lamp on the table, and scattered around it were what looked like sheaves of old paper, a piece of parchment or something, wooden cups, a water pitcher, and various other sundry items. In one corner of the room, more stairs led even further up.

But why hadn't he immediately noticed the person sitting about halfway up that second flight?

Haruhiro backed away, pulling out one of his daggers. He understood now that he was right-handed; he had been holding the lamp in his left hand without realizing why.

Tasukete also lowered his posture, bracing himself. If he'd been carrying a weapon, he would likely have drawn it as well.

The man on the stairs turned to face them. It *was* a man. He didn't look young, but it was hard to place his age. He wore a helmet and armor, with a sword at his hip. The man on the stairs didn't move any further. He was silent, staring at Haruhiro and Tasukete.

"What is this? He's scary..." Tasukete said in a quiet voice.

Haruhiro agreed. The man on the stairs had definitely moved, so he was alive. From all outward appearances, he was human. But was he really? Haruhiro couldn't be sure.

Haruhiro made up his mind. "Hey..." he called out.

The man on the stairs didn't move a muscle. Though, looking closely, Haruhiro could see his shoulders rising and falling slightly. This might seem like it should have been obvious, but he was breathing.

Haruhiro didn't take his eyes off the man on the stairs as he whispered, "Tasukete-san?"

"Huh? Yes?"

"I'm going to test something."

"Test something? Huh? What...?"

"If anything happens, please tell the others."

"You really shouldn't..." Tasukete warned him in a weak voice.

Yeah, maybe I shouldn't, Haruhiro thought, but he fully meant to do it. Was he actually pretty bold? Or just reckless? That wasn't the sense he got. If anything, he thought he might be cautious. Not that he remembered.

Haruhiro approached the table, eyes still on the man on the stairs. The man on the stairs was still not moving. Wait, no—his eyes followed Haruhiro.

Haruhiro laid the lamp down on the table. He tried picking up the parchment, which was apparently a map. The man on the stairs continued scrutinizing him.

Haruhiro took a deep breath. It took some courage, but he sheathed his dagger. The man on the stairs showed no reaction.

Then how about this? Haruhiro rolled up the parchment map with both hands. The man on the stairs still didn't move.

"I'll be borrowing this," Haruhiro said.

There was no response.

"I'm borrowing it," he repeated, backing away with the map in his right hand and the lamp in his left.

Haruhiro passed the map to Tasukete. "Could you hold this for me?"

"Yeah, sure. You've got guts, man..."

"No, I don't. Not really." Haruhiro drew his dagger again. He was pretty sure he was a coward.

This time, he walked all the way around the table. At one point, he got awfully close to the stairs, which naturally meant approaching the man, too, but nothing happened.

He took a quick look at the shelves. There was rope, something that looked like a musical instrument, dried plants, the hide of some small animal, what looked like animal parts, some kind of liquid in a bottle, a small jar, a little box, and some written materials. It looked like similar things had been sorted together, so these things hadn't just been placed here at random. They were organized.

It wasn't clear what was inside the barrels, but it was a liquid—likely alcohol, or oil, or something along those lines. That was the sort of smell it gave off. The ones being used in lieu of chairs were empty.

The wooden boxes were nailed shut. It wouldn't have been impossible to open them if he tried, but Haruhiro decided against it for now. The large jars were stuffed full of meat, fish, or pickled vegetables.

He hadn't thought much of it before now, but the ceiling in this room was pretty high. There were poles stretching across the room at a height that he couldn't reach, and there were sausages hanging from them, as well as smoked fish.

"Is this a warehouse or something?" Haruhiro said to himself. "You could live for a while with all of this..."

The man on the stairs remained unmoving, the same as ever. He just watched Haruhiro intently.

Haruhiro went back to Tasukete.

"It looks like there's more yet," Tasukete said. "I wonder what's here..."

"Who knows?" Haruhiro shook his head. "Let's head back downstairs for now."

Descending the stairs, they told everyone what was on the upper floor. As he spoke, Haruhiro kept a casual eye on Hiyo's reactions. She would go "wow," and "hmm," and "oho," widening her eyes, pursing her lips, and puffing up her cheeks, busily changing her expression. She touched her hair, face, neck, and chest; she shook her head, she blinked repeatedly, she walked around, and she jumped up and down a little. Her gestures were frequent, and all of them were exaggerated.

That seemed concerning to Haruhiro, but maybe his preconceived notions were just making it look that way. All the same, Haruhiro was pretty suspicious of Hiyo, but it was hard to put those suspicions into clear words. He also had a sense that it would be pretty bad if she learned he had any suspicions about her—though he wasn't sure if that was related.

In a word, this was a hunch.

"What should we do?" Haruhiro asked, looking to Kuzaku first.

"Me?" Kuzaku's eyes widened. "Nah, I dunno. Hmmm. What should we do...?"

Haruhiro still didn't really remember Kuzaku, but he figured that was about all he could expect from the guy. *Actually, it might not be the case that I don't remember anything at all,* Haruhiro thought.

For instance, it looked like Shihoru was keeping her head down because she didn't want to be asked for her opinion, but that probably wasn't it; she was desperately trying to think through all this in her own way.

Meanwhile, Setora seemed focused on the handle on the wall. She was sharp. Even if Haruhiro didn't remember that, he felt like he *knew* it.

"Well..." Merry said, lowering her eyes, then a moment later looking over to Hiyo.

Merry was suspicious of Hiyo, like Haruhiro had thought. Though there was one problem with that. Merry was the only one who claimed to have memories right now. If Merry said things were one way or another, Haruhiro and the rest, lacking memories, could only accept that was the way things were. No one could contradict her and say, "That's not right."

What if Merry was lying to them?

Haruhiro did feel like Kuzaku, Shihoru, Setora, Kiichi, and Merry might have been his comrades. But he had no definitive proof of that. Merry said they were volunteer soldiers; Setora was not but was their comrade; and she didn't even know whether Hiyo was a volunteer soldier at all. Haruhiro was starting to believe all of this. But was it actually the *truth*?

Haruhiro thought Hiyo was dubious. But when it came to only remembering their own names, she fell in the same category as Haruhiro and the rest. Merry was the only one with memories. Using those memories, she could provide information, telling Haruhiro and the others, "You are this type of person." Out of all of them, Merry was the only one who could do that. In short, it wasn't impossible to imagine that maybe Merry was the suspicious one here.

However, Merry seemed aware of her unique position. If she set her mind to it, she could weaponize her memories and use them to compel Haruhiro and the rest into doing anything, but she wasn't trying to.

Merry's memories were a double-edged sword. They made a powerful weapon, but if she used them too freely, she would make them all distrust her, and that would lead to her own downfall.

"I'm..." Suddenly, Io crouched. "Hungry."

"Yeah..." Kuzaku held his own stomach. "Me too..."

There was an incredible grumble. That was Gomi's stomach, apparently. "Yeah, seriously. I'm starvin' here..."

"Well, yeeeeaaaah," Hiyo said with a guffaw. "That happens when you're alive. Your belly empties, and empty bellies are inevitable. There's food upstairs, riiiight?"

Come to think of it, Hiyo was the one who had suggested they could go up those stairs in the first place, wasn't she? Was she trying to lead them somewhere? Haruhiro couldn't decide. It was a subtle line.

"There's someone there, though," Haruhiro said.

"But, buuut..." Hiyo looked at them. "There's soooo many of us. If they attack us, can't we just beat the stuffing out of them? Eek! Oh, gosh, Hiyomuuu, you're so violent!"

Shihoru cocked her head to the side. "Hiyomu?"

"Mew?" Hiyo blinked.

"Did I just say that? Did Hiyo just call herself Hiyomu? I wonder why. Is that a nickname? A moniker? A pseudonym? Those are all the same, or close enough, huh? Is that what it is? It could be. Hmmm?" The way Hiyo talked a mile a minute suggested she was not, in fact, mystified by this, but trying to cover her mistake.

Merry looked down, her brow furrowing slightly.

"I don't care what your name is." Io stood up. "Food! We need food! It's like the old saying: 'You can't wage war on an empty stomach!'"

Were they going to wage war? They were called volunteer soldiers, so did they have to fight? Even as Haruhiro thought it, he wasn't so sure about all of that. In any case, he climbed the stairs once more. This time, he was accompanied by everyone, not just Tasukete.

"Huh?"

The room hadn't changed from before, but the man on the stairs had vanished.

"Nobody's here!" Io said in an accusatory tone.

"No, there was before. Really... There was, right?"

When Haruhiro looked to Tasukete for agreement, Tasukete shook his head, seemingly unsure. "I feel like there was. Or maybe...there wasn't..."

"Maybe he went upstairs?" Merry offered helpfully.

Haruhiro nodded. "That's it."

Yeah, he really couldn't doubt Merry.

"Well, whatever the case," Kuzaku said in a reassuring tone, "isn't it better not having some weirdo around? It looks like there's stuff to eat here too."

They spread the map out on the table and looked through the sheaves of paper as they all chewed on sausages and dried fish. They tried opening a barrel, and found that at least one of them contained alcohol. They poured it into cups, and everyone who wanted to drink some did so. Haruhiro tried just a sip, but it was strong stuff, and he'd get drunk off it in no time, so he left it at that.

"This is..." Merry examined the map. "A map of Grimgar, maybe?"

"Grimgar?" Haruhiro felt he had heard that name, or maybe not, but it sounded not entirely unfamiliar.

"This is Alterna," Merry said, pointing to the lower part of the map. "North of here is the Quickwind Plains. Then there's the Shadow Forest where the elves live, and far to the east is the sea. Here. This is the free city of Vele."

"Alterna... Elves... Vele... Free city..." Haruhiro didn't know any of these words. Yet, at the same time, he felt like he'd heard them before.

If he ran into a person, he might see them from behind and think he knew them. But if he couldn't see their face, he couldn't be absolutely sure they were someone he knew.

It was like that now. These words weren't completely unknown to him. He did know them. Or he had known them, but he'd forgotten. But for something he'd forgotten... The more he thought about it, the more his head hurt.

It was an unpleasant pain too. Where was this pain coming from? Probably deep inside his head. It wasn't a stabbing pain, or a throbbing one. It was a little like an itch, but it felt *unbearably* itchy.

"We set out from Vele..." Merry pointed to a spot on the map. She moved her finger to the left. "We were heading to Alterna, but along the way we ran into...a camp... Right, it was Ainrand Leslie's camp—the Leslie Camp."

"It's no good." Setora crossed her arms and frowned. "I can't remember it at all."

"Oh!" Kuzaku still had a sausage in his mouth. "Was this including me too? I was listening like it was about someone else..."

Io had a look on her face that was difficult to read. "The Leslie Camp...?"

"What is thaaat?" Hiyo asked with a smile. "This, ummmm? Wrestling champ, was it?"

Merry looked Hiyo in the eye. Hiyo's expression tensed a little. Or that was how it seemed to Haruhiro.

"From there," Merry continued without responding to Hiyo's question, "We wandered into another world. It was like a really bad dream had become reality..."

Hiyo stroked her chin. "Hmmm." Her eyes went up and to the right. "Y'know, if it was like a bad dream, that makes me think that maaaaybe it really was a dream? Oh, not that I'm doubting you or anythiiiing."

"You could be right." Merry looked down at the map. "It might all have been a dream I saw. Even now, I'm sort of wondering if the dream just hasn't ended yet."

"That's not it," Haruhiro said definitively.

He said this without meaning to, and now Merry, Hiyo, and everyone else looked at him.

Haruhiro scratched his head and looked to the side. "I don't think that's how it is. If I were just a character in Merry's dream, I dunno... I wouldn't be able to think for myself or act alone, right? Probably not. But I am. I am... Or at least, I'm trying to."

"Me too. Me too," Kuzaku said with a chuckle.

"Don't imitate me..."

"No, I'm not imitating you. I'm saying I think you're right!"

"Like! I! Said!" Hiyo put her hands on her hips and puffed up her cheeks. "It's not like I'm doubting you or anythiiiing."

"Merry-san, if your memories are right..." Shihoru leaned in, looking closely at the map. "Where would we be now?"

Haruhiro looked around the room. This room and the one below had no windows. It went without saying that they were in a building, but what was it like outside? Like Shihoru was asking, where exactly were they?

"The handle..." Tasukete said in a small voice.

It immediately occurred to Haruhiro that he meant the handle on the wall downstairs. That handle had caught his attention the moment he saw it. If Hiyo hadn't suggested they could go up the stairs, Haruhiro might have tried pulling that handle like a lever first.

"I'm going back downstairs. I'm going to try that handle. It might do something," Haruhiro declared.

At this, Hiyo looked somewhat unamused, then let out a sigh. Haruhiro was almost certain: Hiyo was a liar.

The question was what she was lying about, and why?

Grimgar of Fantasy and Ash

2 | Red Moon Rhapsody

HARUHIRO had everyone back away close to the staircase for safety, then he went to stand in front of the lever alone.

Kuzaku offered to do it, but Haruhiro turned him down. It wasn't that he didn't trust Kuzaku to handle things, it was just that he couldn't help but feel this was something he ought to do himself.

Haruhiro remained alert, and he tried to emotionally prepare himself, but it probably wasn't a trap. There wasn't likely to be an explosion, or poison gas, or anything dangerous like that when he pulled the lever. When he looked at the handle, the base of it, and the wall around it, Haruhiro got the sense that it was safe. Tasukete seemed to agree.

This was something his experience as a thief told him. He didn't remember any of that experience, but clearly those memories weren't gone entirely.

Haruhiro grabbed the handle. His grip wasn't exactly relaxed, but his fingers weren't overly tense either. He gently pulled it down.

There was a click, like something falling into place. Shortly afterward, a portion of the wall began to sink with a dull grinding noise.

"So that's how it works."

Though he hadn't been anticipating any danger, he was still a little relieved. It was a hidden door. Where did it lead? A somewhat chilly draft came into the room. Wind. He felt a slight breeze.

Kuzaku and the others came over. "Outside?" Kuzaku put a hand on Haruhiro's shoulder. "It leads outside, doesn't it? Outside! We can get outside!"

Outside, outside. Would you shut up? Haruhiro smiled a little. "Looks like it."

He subtly glanced over at Hiyo's face. She was expressionless. It was like she wasn't thinking or feeling anything as she looked past the hidden door.

Merry tried to head outside. Haruhiro stopped her. "Hold on."

Merry seemed to come to her senses as she turned to Haruhiro, then nodded. They waited for the hidden door to open fully, then Haruhiro went ahead on his own.

It wasn't pitch dark. The distant horizon was still bright, so maybe the dawn was coming. Or the sun had just set. He turned to look back and a tower loomed over him. They had been inside of it.

Haruhiro was, for obvious reasons, confused. But considering he was able to recognize his own confusion, he figured he was still managing to keep his cool.

There was a slight orange hue to the horizon, but what direction was that? If it was west, it was sunset. If it was east, it was sunrise.

The moon hung in the sky above. From where Haruhiro stood, the right side of it was occluded, but was it a waxing crescent moon, or a waning crescent moon?

"It's red..."

Something about that bothered him. The moon. The *red* moon. Wait... Was the moon red? Of course it was red. If it wasn't red, what was it?

Kuzaku and the others came out of the tower.

"This is..." Merry turned to look up at the tower. "The Forbidden Tower..."

The tower stood on a hill. It was a grassy slope, dotted with white stones. They looked like graves. Perhaps this hill was a graveyard, and the Forbidden Tower which stood at its peak was a massive gravestone.

"A town, huh?" Setora said, and Kiichi meowed.

Setora was looking past the hill. Was that a town? It probably was. There were tens, or hundreds, or perhaps even more buildings surrounded by high walls. Though quite sparse, there were lights there, too, which reassured Haruhiro for some reason.

No, there was no need to wonder about the reason. He was reassured because there was a town right there.

"Alterna." Merry spoke an unfamiliar word.

Haruhiro didn't know it, but he couldn't say for certain that he had never heard it before. Alterna. It was probably not completely unrelated to the town down there. It had to be the town's name. He tried saying it for himself. "Alterna."

Would a feeling of nostalgia well up inside him? He kind of

hoped it would. Sadly, he felt nothing. The lack of emotion left him somewhat despondent.

"This is where it all began," Merry said to no one in particular. "We're finally back. We took quite the detour, though."

Haruhiro looked at Alterna once more. Yeah, he really wasn't feeling anything. Kuzaku, Shihoru, Io, Gomi, Tasukete, and Setora were also looking toward Alterna.

"Le sigh…" Hiyo was alone in gazing up at the red moon, her brow knitted. "Weeeell, there goes that plan. Hrmm. Y'know? Sometimes things just don't go how you expect, huh? Seriously. I dunno what to do. Should I report back to Master? Is he gonna get mad at me for this? It's not Hiyomu's fault, though. Hiyomu didn't mess it up, okay? If anything, Hiyomu's the victim here…"

At this point, no one was looking at Alterna. Everyone, even Kiichi, was staring at Hiyo in blank amazement.

"Hahh…" Hiyo let out another big sigh. Then her eyes swept across Haruhiro and the rest. Her personality seemed to have changed completely. There was something sharp and toxic about the look she gave them.

"Okay, okay, okaaaay." Hiyo clapped her hands twice. "Is everyone ready? Even if you aren't, you should listen reeeeal good. Hiyomu's about to tell you something *important*. If you miss it, you're gonna regret it, like, terribad."

Her tone was different. It was the same voice as before, obviously, but lower. This tone, though filled with menace, might have been more natural for her.

"You all have a choiiiice to make. Two options. First." Hiyo brought her right hand forward, raising her index finger. "You can listen to Hiyomu. I'm not saying you have to be Hiyomu's slave or anything. Buuuut, you do have to follow Hiyomu's master's orders, okay? It's all upsides, really. He's a great master to serve. I mean, Hiyomu swore her loyalty to him, so that should tell you just how great a master he is, right?"

"What are you talking..." Io started to say, then trailed off and fell silent.

"And?" Setora asked in a completely calm voice. "What is the second option?"

"Secoooond." Hiyo raised the index finger of her left hand. "If you won't do what Hiyomu tells you, then you can go do whatever the hell you want. Though, in exchange, I won't be telling you a single thing about the mystery of this world and the truth behind it, okay? You'll be back at the beginning, thrown out into Grimgar with nothing but yourselves to rely on."

"The...mystery of this world?" Merry's voice sounded hoarse. "The truth...? You know that?"

"Did you think I'd answer if you asked me, hmmmm?" Hiyo snorted. "Don't misunderstand. I don't like your attitude. It's crap. Utter crap. Something reeks about you. Maybe because *you're* a piece of crap, you bitch."

"Somebody's got a foul mouth..." Kuzaku sounded a little sad.

"Oh, yeah?" Hiyo kept going. "Well, Hiyomu's master possesses incredible knowledge and near-immortality. He has treasures beyond counting in his collection. He is a great, great sage who's learned all the mysteries of this world, and with his amassed wisdom,

he *obviously* knows anything and everything you could possibly want to learn. Not that you'd know that, because you people don't even remember anything. You're not *supposed* to remember!"

"What you're saying is that the reason we lost our memories," Setora plainly pointed out, "is because you—no, your master did something to us."

Hiyo neither confirmed nor denied this. She smiled slightly as she pushed her two index fingers together. Then, shifting in an instant, she glared at Merry and demanded, "You can't possibly remember, so what's with you?"

"What's with me? I'm..." Merry backed away. Her voice was trembling. No, not just her voice. Her body too. Merry shook her head repeatedly. Again, and again, and again. "I... I'm..."

"This is going nowhere." Hiyo sounded irritated, and she clicked her tongue repeatedly. "Whatever the case, you all need to make a choice. I mean, you should be beside yourselves with gratitude that I'm even giving you a choice at all."

Haruhiro was taken aback. The change was so sudden and complete.

No, he didn't have time to be surprised. They were being pushed to make a choice. They had to choose here and now. There were two options: Obey Hiyo—a.k.a. Hiyomu—or don't. Did they really have to choose?

Like he'd expected, Hiyomu was a suspicious individual. Haruhiro had no idea how they could have done it, but it was possible that she—or her master, whoever that was—might have been the ones who stole their memories.

Which meant what? They were the victims, and Hiyomu was the perpetrator. Why did the victims have to do what the person who had harmed them said?

Haruhiro was getting a little angry. Did Hiyomu have any right to make demands of them? She didn't, did she?

Kuzaku looked like he was getting mad too. "Now, listen!" he shouted, rounding on Hiyomu.

That was the moment it happened. Hiyomu whipped her headpiece, or hairpiece, or whatever it was off her head, and threw it at Kuzaku. "Don't move, dimwit!"

It was a small thing, less than fist-sized, and it looked like a stuffed animal. It didn't look like it would do anything if it hit him.

But when it struck Kuzaku square in the chest, he let out a groan and fell on his backside so fast it looked like he might flip over. On top of that, the thing bounced once, twice, then returned to rest firmly in Hiyomu's right hand.

Hiyomu turned to Setora, Gomi, and Haruhiro, making a menacing gesture like she was about to throw it again, then chuckled to herself. "Don't you dare underestimate the Paw of Terror. Master gave me this relic. Hiyomu's the one who named it, though, okay?"

Kuzaku was still sputtering and coughing. He pressed down on his chest where the Paw of Terror—or whatever she wanted to call that thing—had struck him. "Ow, that hurt!"

It looked like it had done some serious damage. If Kuzaku wasn't exaggerating, it might have even busted a rib.

"Annnnd." Hiyomu tossed the Paw of Terror up a little, then caught it as it came back down. "This isn't Hiyomu's only weapon. Now, some of you lowlifes might think I'm bluffing when I say that, but I'm not. Hiyomu's a relic master who serves as one of Master's disciples, so murdering you all would be a piece of cake. I'm telling the truth here, okay? You wanna try me? Maybe I'll kill one of you to make a point?"

That honestly sounded dubious. Haruhiro didn't know what a relic master was supposed to be, but Hiyomu didn't seem to have much other than that Paw of Terror on her. Still, she might only be making it look that way. She could still be hiding some seriously crazy weapons.

"Okay." Io stepped forward. Her chest was thrust out and her chin was raised slightly so she could look down on whomever she spoke to, despite her small stature. "I'll obey you. No matter who it is that's responsible for this, the fact is that we have no memories. You have to be joking if you think I'm going to wander around with no idea what to do, or even what's going on, and then just die somewhere."

Hiyomu grinned. "That intelligence will take you a long way. Not with Hiyomu, but with Hiyomu's master."

Io shrugged, then turned back and surveyed Haruhiro and the others. "What about the rest of you?"

"M-me too." Tasukete stepped forward, his eyes lowered. "I think I'll obey..."

"I hate yer guts," Gomi said, glaring at Hiyomu. "But still, I'm, uh...Io's—"

"Io-sama," Io corrected him with a voice like an icy whip, "is what you are to call me. It's beyond upsetting that a man like you would address me without an honorific, but if you could show me the proper respect and call me 'Io-sama,' I wouldn't be completely unable to put up with you."

"I-Io-sama's..." Gomi twisted his neck to look at Merry. "Comrade... That was it, right? Was that even true?"

Merry had an awkward look on her face. "Supposedly."

"Righty-o, let Hiyomu tell you the answeeeer." Hiyomu said in a tone that was more silly than relaxed. "Gomi-kun and Tasukete-kun *were* Io-chan's comrades. Io-chan went around making her comrades call her Io-sama. You all made a name for yourselves as the Io-sama Squad."

"The Io-sama...Squad..." Gomi clutched his head.

"I was...Io-sama's...?" Tasukete looked at Io through his bangs. "Io-sama..."

"I know a whole lot more, too," Hiyomu said with a nasty smile. "With Master's permission, I could tell you a little at a time. You can switch from being the used to being the users. Let me tell you, this is a once-in-a-lifetime opportunity here. Turn it down, and you are soooo going to regret it."

Haruhiro turned his eyes toward Kuzaku. Kuzaku was still down on the ground. Was he dumbfounded by all this?

Next, Haruhiro looked at Shihoru's expression. Shihoru had her chin lowered and was looking at Hiyomu with narrowed eyes.

He had no idea what Setora was thinking, but she hadn't moved at all. Kiichi was at her feet, staying put.

"Merry," Haruhiro called out to her.

"Huh?" Merry looked at Haruhiro with surprise. "What?"

Haruhiro nodded to her. Even without putting it into words, he felt like she'd understand what he meant. It looked like she got it. Merry nodded back to him.

"As for us," Haruhiro said, then rubbed his nose. He'd thought he was sweating there, but he wasn't. It was strangely cool. Was he feeling tense, or not? He wasn't quite sure.

Haruhiro took a breath, then looked at Hiyomu again. "We won't obey you. Sorry to turn down your no doubt wonderful offer, but we're going to do what we want."

"Oh, myyy." Hiyomu put on a smile that didn't extend beyond her lips, narrowing her eyes unhappily, then swung the Paw of Terror.

Haruhiro moved as if he'd anticipated it. By the time Hiyomu threw the paw, Haruhiro had already jumped on Merry and pushed her down.

"Whaa?!" Hiyomu cried out in shock.

Hiyomu had thrown the paw at Merry, not Haruhiro. Based on how it flew, if Haruhiro hadn't pushed Merry down, she'd have been in trouble. The Paw of Terror might have struck her right in the face.

"Nnnnnngh!" Hiyomu ground her teeth, then took off running. "We're going, Io-sama Squad! Follow Hiyomu!"

"I guess we have no choice, huh?" Io followed. After a beat, Gomi and Tasukete ran after them.

"Wait, you forgot this!" Shihoru grabbed the cloak that was

covering her. She might have been about to take it off, but she stopped just short of doing so.

Still running, Gomi turned back to look. "You can have it! Wear the damn thing!"

The ominously dark-colored cloak that Shihoru was wearing had belonged to Gomi.

The four who left headed back for the Forbidden Tower. It all happened so quickly.

"Ugh..." someone groaned underneath Haruhiro. No, it wasn't just someone, it was Merry. Right. He'd pushed her down and hadn't moved since. Uh-oh.

"I-I'm sor—" he tried to apologize as he got off her, but she pushed him away before he could finish. "Huh?!"

When Merry jumped to her feet, the fingers of her right hand were already moving. She drew some kind of pictures, or figures, or sigils in the air as she chanted.

"Marc em parc."

Something like a bead of light appeared in front of Merry's chest. It started off smaller than a fist but grew visibly as Haruhiro watched.

Hiyomu turned back. "Huh?!" Her eyes went wide. "Magic Missile?!"

The bead of light, now larger than a person's head, flew toward Hiyomu.

"Waaaaaagh!" Hiyomu let out a weird scream.

"Seriously?!" Gomi turned and pulled out a big sword.

For a moment, it looked as if Gomi had disappeared. Maybe

he just moved that fast? Then Gomi slashed his sword through the bead of light that was about to clobber Hiyomu.

Oh, I guess that's something you can cut after all, Haruhiro thought.

It was light, after all. Could you cut sunlight with a kitchen knife? No way. But Gomi's sword cleaved the bead of light cleanly in two. Once it was bisected, the bead vanished without a trace.

"The hell was that?!" Gomi shouted, holding his sword at the ready.

Having just been saved by Gomi, Hiyomu stared at Merry. "Y-y-you're a priest, but you just used m-m-magic..."

Io and Tasukete just stood there.

Haruhiro looked at Merry. She was clutching her head, as if trying to tear her own hair out. Something was weird. Her face was distorted and her teeth were clenched. It looked like she was suffering badly.

"Merry?" he asked.

"It's fine," Merry responded immediately, but she didn't look fine at all.

The Paw of Terror hopped along on its own until it returned to Hiyomu's hands. "I'm gonna have to take this one to Master right away. It's weird enough she hasn't lost her memories, but now she's started using magic too. Besides, that Magic Missile was beyond anything your average mage could do."

Was Merry still struggling? Her face was turned down, but she was still glaring at Hiyomu, and her lips were moving. Was she muttering something? Haruhiro couldn't hear her voice.

Hiyomu waved her arm without another word, and when Io and her group noticed, they took off at a jog. Hiyomu also headed for the Forbidden Tower, keeping a wary eye on Merry as she went.

Haruhiro and the others stood there in silence, not moving until the four were inside the tower. Not long after they were out of sight, something about the Forbidden Tower changed.

"Ah!" Kuzaku cried out when he realized. "The entrance..."

They had pulled the lever to close the secret entrance. If there was no other way in, Haruhiro and the others wouldn't be able to enter the tower.

"Hmm," Setora nodded. "I see. It only opens from the inside. So that's why it's called the Forbidden Tower."

"Is now the time to be thinking about that?" Kuzaku asked.

Shihoru hesitantly walked over to Merry and took a closer look at her face. "Um... Merry-san?"

Merry shook her head, then smiled at Shihoru. "Merry is fine. That's what I asked you to call me before." It was an obviously forced smile.

The sky was getting brighter. It wasn't dusk. It was dawn. Haruhiro looked toward the walled city. "Alterna, huh?"

Grimgar of Fantasy and Ash

3 | The Second Time

HOW LONG had that tower on the hill near Alterna stood there? Merry said she didn't know. Regardless, volunteer soldiers called it the Forbidden Tower, or "the tower that never opens." They couldn't go inside it, so it was more of a landmark than anything else.

If one were to be precise, it only forbade entrance from the outside, and it opened just fine from the inside, so it was really "the tower that never lets people in."

"Anyway, why don't we try going to Alterna?"

No one objected to Setora's suggestion.

Haruhiro began descending the well-trodden dirt path. It led from the Forbidden Tower to the bottom of the hill, then on to Alterna. There were grassy fields on either side, each of them dotted with large white stones. He asked Merry about these, and it turned out they were graves, like he had guessed.

"They're almost all graves for volunteer soldiers... Comrades of ours are sleeping here too."

"Whoa..." Kuzaku was speechless.

"But without any memories, we can't exactly mourn them, now, can we?" Setora didn't hold back.

Shihoru came to a stop, and for a little while she looked around the graveyard, as if searching for something, but when Haruhiro called her name, she started walking again.

Haruhiro wondered about his erstwhile comrades now sleeping beneath these graves. When things settled down, maybe he'd have to ask Merry where their graves were and pay them a visit. Though, like Setora said, there was no way he could mourn their loss when he didn't even remember them, so it felt kind of pointless visiting their graves.

"Can we get in?" Kuzaku asked himself in a whisper.

The stone walls surrounding Alterna were easily twice the height of a person, and the gate up ahead was closed.

"The first bell in Alterna chimes at six in the morning," Merry told them. "The gate should open after that."

The sun was almost up, but there were still watch fires lit here and there along the walls of Alterna. Were there guards posted? There were humanoid figures standing on top of the wall.

"Six in the morning, huh...?" Haruhiro said, then placed his hand lightly on his chest.

Was he imagining this? No, he wasn't. It wasn't his imagination. There was something making his heart race. He just couldn't put his finger on what it was.

"So, you people are volunteer soldiers, right?" Setora asked Merry. "Who exactly were you fighting against?"

Merry thought about that for a moment. "To sum it all up in one group, the Alliance of Kings. Arabakia, the kingdom of the human race, was attacked by the orcs, undead, goblins, and kobolds. They lost this land, which we now call the frontier."

"Hmm." Kuzaku cocked his head to the side. "Then, Arabakia's enemies—our enemies—aren't human?"

Merry nodded. "They're primarily orcs and undead."

"Well, compared to fighting humans, that's... You know? Well, maybe you don't know. But still."

Haruhiro came to a stop. "They're...not human..."

"Huh?" Kuzaku stopped too. "What?"

Haruhiro squinted as he looked up at the top of the walls. There were silhouettes up there. Some moving, some not. The wall was still over a hundred meters away, and he didn't really have enough light, so he couldn't make the shapes out clearly. But from what he could see, they were increasing in number. There were a large number of guards up on the wall, and they were gradually gathering.

Kiichi let out a short, sharp hiss. He was facing the wall, his thick tail raised. No, it wasn't just his tail—every hair on Kiichi's body was raised.

"It's kind of like..." Haruhiro struggled to find the words. He didn't really know what it was, so he'd just have to say exactly what he was thinking. "We're being watched...?"

The next moment, a voice cried, "Whooaaaahhh!" It came

from the direction of the wall. He thought it was a voice, at least. It was pretty throaty.

"They're not human," Haruhiro repeated.

Yeah. They weren't human. That was it. The silhouettes on the wall looked human at a distance. Their figures seemed humanoid, at least, but there was something strange about them.

It was just that, well, they were all a bit small. They wore helmets and armor and whatnot, but they were too small to be adults. They were like a troop of children.

Eventually, a sound like the beating of metal on metal rang out. Clang, clang, clang! The guards who looked like child soldiers began hooting and hollering.

"Those voices..." Merry shook her head. "No way... It can't be. How...?"

Something came flying at them from the wall.

"What's that?" Kuzaku asked.

"Get back!" Haruhiro screamed instinctively.

A great number of thin, stick-like objects were launched from the wall, tracing a large arc through the air before raining down on the group.

Every single one of them turned heel at practically the same time. Haruhiro heard the thin objects slamming into the earth behind them. As he ran, he unconsciously found himself checking for Kuzaku, Shihoru, Merry, Setora, and Kiichi. It looked like they were all fine.

"Alterna's out!" Merry said. "There're enemies inside!"

"Enemies?!" Kuzaku shouted. "What does that mean?!"

"I don't know!" Merry shouted back.

Without stopping, Setora looked behind her. "This doesn't look like the time to argue."

More of the thin objects came flying toward them. Those were arrows. Ten, twenty, maybe more of them. It looked like the group was already out of range, so the arrows didn't reach them this time.

Still, the gates of Alterna were opening. They weren't fully open yet, but the army of children was pouring out through them. Okay, it was clear it was not, in fact, an army of child soldiers, but what were they, then?

Enemies. That was what Merry had called them. They were enemies. Simple as that.

Haruhiro and the others climbed the hill. The Forbidden Tower stood atop it.

"If we can get in there!" he shouted. *That would be great, but it's not happening, huh?*

Hiyomu had made them an offer, telling them to submit to her, and had said they would definitely regret it if they didn't. This must have been what she meant.

According to Merry's story, Alterna was a town of the Kingdom of Arabakia, where Haruhiro and the others served as volunteer soldiers, but that had changed now. Something had happened, and the town was occupied by enemies.

They shouldn't have approached Alterna so carelessly. It had made it easy for the enemy to find them. And what would happen if an enemy found you? This. They would be shot at with arrows and chased after.

"Damn her!"

Still, no matter how Haruhiro cursed at Hiyomu, who was no doubt kicking back and relaxing inside the Forbidden Tower right now, she couldn't hear him. It wouldn't improve the situation either.

Maybe because she had nothing on under her cloak, Shihoru seemed to be having a hard time running, and she'd fallen a bit behind. Haruhiro slowed his pace and waited for her to catch up.

"Can you keep running?!"

Shihoru nodded, but her breathing was ragged, and she didn't exactly pick up the pace. Was this too hard on her? He tried shouting, "You can do this!" but all that did was make Shihoru nod again.

It wasn't just enemy soldiers who had come out of the gates. There were smaller creatures with them too. What were those things? They were barking, so dogs, maybe? There weren't that many of them. Two—no, three of the blackish dogs were chasing after them.

Kuzaku was saying something like, "Oh crap, oh crap, oh crap."

The dogs were faster than the soldiers. They were rapidly gaining on Haruhiro and the others. If it were just the enemy soldiers, they might have been able to shake them, but the dogs were eventually going to catch up.

They were almost at the summit. Setora and Kiichi were already by the Forbidden Tower.

"What now?!" Setora shouted.

The dogs had closed in and were only two, three meters away from Haruhiro and Shihoru.

"Merry?!"

Was there no safe place other than Alterna? Merry, who still had her memories, was the only one they could rely on here.

"Sorry!" Merry frowned. "I don't know either!"

Haruhiro would have been lying if he claimed he wasn't thinking, *We're screwed*. Still, he changed gears in an instant and quickly surveyed his surroundings.

The sun was rising in the east, so that line of really high mountains must have been to the south, right? There was a forest spreading out to the north.

"Head for the forest—" was all he managed to get out before the dog lunged.

Haruhiro reflexively put his left arm in front of himself, trying to guard. The dog bit that arm at his left wrist.

"Oh!" The attack surprised him, and he was scared, but at the same time, he retained the composure to think, *This dog's pretty small*. It wasn't just small; its legs were tiny too. If this were a big dog, it would have bowled him over, or at least pushed him down. It still had a strong bite, though.

"That hurts!" Haruhiro let the dog bite his left wrist, then pummeled it in the head with his right fist.

The dog yelped and loosened its bite. Taking advantage of that opening, Haruhiro shook it off him.

"Ah!" Shihoru screamed.

Another dog had leapt on her when she tripped. Haruhiro

didn't hesitate to kick the dog in the side, getting it off of Shihoru. Immediately after that, yet another dog bit Haruhiro, this time in the shin.

"I said, that hurts!" Haruhiro pulled his dagger from the sheath at his hip. He wasn't exactly enraged, but he didn't hesitate to slash the dog's throat.

Copious amounts of blood gushed from the wound. Haruhiro hadn't just cut the dog's carotid artery, he'd torn open its trachea too. It was still alive for now, but it couldn't breathe anymore. When Haruhiro shook his right leg, the dog lost its grip and fell to the ground.

The remaining two mutts yelped noisily, but maybe what had happened to their friend had them scared, because they didn't attack.

Haruhiro pulled Shihoru to her feet.

"Haruhiro-kun, a-are you hurt?!"

"I think I'm probably fine. This is no big deal. You?"

"I-I'm okay."

"Well, go on ahead, then."

Haruhiro gave Shihoru a push in the right direction. He had another dagger. He drew it, and the blade was like a dancing flame. When he held both blades with a backhand grip, it was strange how right that felt for him.

He paused and took a breath. He had two dogs barking at him, and enemy soldiers closing in, but Haruhiro wasn't all that flustered. No, actually, he wasn't flustered in the slightest.

The enemy had yellowish-green skin, and the faces peering

out through the openings in their helms were clearly not human. They stood two heads shorter than Haruhiro. Kuzaku was a pretty tall guy, but Haruhiro was probably of average height, so it was safe to say they were about the size of a human child.

There were more than ten of them—no, more than fifteen, but less than twenty. He caught himself thinking *That's a few too many,* then nearly laughed at how crazy that was. A few? It was way too many. He was more than just outnumbered, so what did he think he was doing? Why would he do this?

He had to let Shihoru get away. He had to save his comrade. His comrade? Even though he didn't remember her? It felt stupid, but he had no regrets. Actually, it felt good.

Haruhiro charged the enemy soldiers. They must not have been expecting him to come at them alone, so that put them on the back foot a little.

I'd better take out one or two now. That was the thought that crossed Haruhiro's mind.

What crossed his sight, though, was something else entirely.

"Hahhhh!"

Kuzaku really was tall. He wasn't fat, but he had broad shoulders and a thick chest, so he looked absolutely huge. Especially when his opponents were so little.

Kuzaku jumped right in front of Haruhiro from the side, swinging down with his big sword. He cut one enemy from shoulder to flank, literally slicing him in two.

"Haruhiro! Going it alone like this!" Kuzaku stepped in farther with a big swing of his sword. Big, but not random or without thought. As proof of that, Kuzaku's blade cut down another enemy. "You're trying to be too cool! So you should really stop!"

The enemy were noticeably intimidated. Well, after seeing Kuzaku pull that trick, could you really blame them?

"No, man, you're being way cooler, you know?"

"Huh? You think so?" Kuzaku got a goofy grin on his face, but then cut down yet another enemy. "Is this nuts or what? Maybe I'm strong?"

"They're just goblins, but there's a lot of them!" Merry shouted as she ran over. "Push in and finish this quickly!"

It looked like Kuzaku wasn't the only one who had turned around and come back rather than fleeing.

"O Light, may Lumiaris's divine protection be upon you." Merry pressed her right hand to her forehead, then thrust her hand out toward the enemy. "Blame!"

There was a powerful flash from Merry's hand, and the enemies were sent flying.

Setora picked up an *enemy's* fallen spear and thrust it at another *enemy*. When it impaled that *enemy's* throat, Setora let go of it without even trying to pull it out. Then, as if saying *I've got my weapon right here,* she snatched up the impaled *enemy's* axe and threw it at yet another *enemy*. The axe spun through the air before burying itself in that enemy's chest. Right after that, another *enemy* tried to attack Setora, but Kiichi pounced on him. The new *enemy* had a helmet that covered his entire head, but Kiichi quickly and skillfully tore it off, then sank his claws into the *enemy's* eyes.

As that was happening, Kuzaku was cutting down enemies one after another.

The two dogs just kept barking. One enemy fled, practically rolling down the hill. That caused the rest of the enemies to suddenly break, and the dogs followed them in their scattered retreat.

Kuzaku started to give chase, but before Haruhiro had time to stop him, Kuzaku stopped himself. It seemed he hadn't meant to seriously pursue them, just to send the message: *I'm gonna come after you!* He then turned to Haruhiro and said, "Now's our chance!"

Haruhiro nodded. For his own part, he shouted, "To the forest!" but he couldn't help but think, *Did I really have to say that?* Everyone—even Shihoru, who was far from nimble—was already heading toward the forest. It seemed it might be the case that they'd all had a lot of experiences like this before they lost their memories, and their bodies still remembered, even if their minds didn't.

The group rushed down the hill and into the northern woods.

There was no guarantee that there wouldn't be reinforcements coming from Alterna, but it didn't look like they were being pursued for now.

"This forest isn't so big," Merry told them.

They went about three hundred meters into the trees before stopping for a rest.

"Now then..." Setora was holding a spear she had seized from the enemy. It was about as long as she was tall—which, incidentally, was a little shorter than Haruhiro. "What exactly was that all about? Goblins, I think you called them?"

"Yes."

According to Merry, those enemies belonged to a race known as goblins. They were part of the Alliance of Kings. Naturally, they were hostile to the Kingdom of Arabakia, and they were based out of a place to the northwest called Damuro.

"So this, uh, Damuro place?" Kuzaku asked, scratching his neck. "The goblins from there attacked Alterna, and took it, or something like that? I mean, there were a lot of them just now, but they were pretty weak. So the Kingdom of Arabakia, was it? They lost to those things?"

Shihoru hung her head. "I couldn't do anything. I was just in the way..."

"You were a mage," Setora said with a shrug. "You'll just have to remember your magic, won't you?"

"Nyaa," Kiichi meowed. He was looking at Shihoru, not his master, Setora. He might have been trying to encourage her.

"Speaking of magic..." Kuzaku looked at Merry. "Merry-san, didn't you use something like magic? Can Shihoru-san do stuff like that?"

Merry lowered her eyes. "What I use is the priest's light magic."

You mean that "marc em parc" stuff? Haruhiro considered asking that for a moment, but something stopped him. Why did he stop? He didn't really know that himself. No, that was a lie. It wasn't like he had no idea why.

Merry had drawn some sort of figure in the air with her fingers as she chanted "Marc em parc," and it had produced a bead of light. She'd tried to hit Hiyomu with it. That had really surprised Hiyomu, and unless Haruhiro was misremembering, she'd said *"You're a priest, but you just used magic."*

Hiyomu had seemed familiar with everyone's backgrounds, not just Io and her group's. Despite that, when Merry used that spell, it had caught Hiyomu by surprise. Didn't that mean that Merry shouldn't have been able to use that magic?

Besides, Merry had been acting strangely then, even if Haruhiro found it hard to explain exactly how. He didn't remember what Merry had been like before this, so he was having a hard time being confident of that, but there was something about it that made him go, "Huh?"

"By light magic, you mean this?" Setora thrust her hand forward to demonstrate. "You blew the goblins away with light."

Merry nodded. "Blame is about the only attack spell I have. But I can use a number of spells that heal wounds. As long as something's not instantly fatal, I can generally take care of it."

"Ooh." Kuzaku's eyes widened. "That's reassuring."

"You're a paladin, Kuzaku, so you can use light magic too. It's a little different from a priest's, though."

"Huh? Me too? Seriously? Sweet! Oh, but I can't remember it, though..."

Setora twirled her spear and thrust the blunt end of it lightly into the ground. "It seems I can do enough to look after myself, at least."

"You were always able to do a bit of everything," Merry said. "You were a necromancer, and a nyaa master. You could use a range of weapons too. But above all that, you were smarter than most people."

This much praise was bound to make a person feel embarrassed, but Setora seemed unfazed. "I understand that's how you saw me. I'm sure the reality was quite different, though."

"Whoa." Kuzaku stared at Setora. "You're pretty awesome, huh, Setora-san?"

"You remind me of a dog, somehow," she responded.

"Whaa? How?"

"The way you act so clingy and excessively friendly is just like a dog."

"I'm not really being excessively friendly, and I'm not clinging to you either. I'm keeping my distance, see?"

"If you weren't, I'd either punch or kick you."

"Harsh..."

Haruhiro had just killed one of the goblins' dogs, so he had a hard time seeing Kuzaku as dog-like. Still, it was true that Kuzaku reminded him of a friendly dog in some ways.

Honestly, it was a big help having Kuzaku around. The way Kuzaku had mowed down enemies in battle made him reliable; that went without saying. But on top of that, while Kuzaku could be a little annoying—though that might only be because Haruhiro didn't have his memories of their time as comrades—Haruhiro found the overly familiar way in which Kuzaku interacted with him comforting.

It wasn't clear what Hiyomu's master, whoever that was, had done to them, but between the lack of memories and Alterna being in the state it was, nothing good had come of it. Kuzaku being here with him might have been the only reason that Haruhiro felt like they could still manage, despite their losses.

Obviously, Merry having maintained her memories was a large part of it too.

"Um, I had a question," Shihoru said hesitantly. "You said we were volunteer soldiers... Does that mean we volunteered? I can't imagine I'm cut out for this..."

"That's..." Merry hesitated. "I think we were left with no other option."

"No other option?" Haruhiro parroted back. "What do you mean by that...?"

"This is probably the second time."

"For what?"

"Not for Setora and Kiichi, but for the rest of us, this isn't the first time we've lost our memories."

Haruhiro rubbed his cheeks. "The second time."

Merry nodded. "Yes."

Grimgar
of
Fantasy and Ash

4 | The Dark Is Cold and Gentle

THE FIRST TIME...

When she came to, Merry had nothing but the clothes she happened to be wearing, and she remembered nothing beyond her own name.

Merry was not alone; she was in a group of eleven people, and out of those eleven, the ones she ended up working with were Hayashi, Michiki, Ogu, and Mutsumi.

Though Merry didn't remember the experience clearly, Hiyomu had suddenly shown up and led them to Alterna. That must have happened in front of the Forbidden Tower, because she had no memories of Hiyomu below or inside the tower.

When Merry told this story, Haruhiro noticed something. For some reason, the details of his time inside of the tower and the area beneath it were a haze. He checked with Kuzaku, Shihoru, and Setora, and it was the same for all of them.

As Merry explained it, the memories would come back, like, "Oh, yeah, that's what it was like." But when he tried to recall the finer details of that place on his own, he just couldn't seem to. The conversations he'd had inside and below the tower were kind of a blur.

"Maybe we were drugged," Setora suggested.

According to Setora, though she couldn't remember the specific types, the secretions of certain plants and animals could cause hallucinations, hypnosis, and derangement. It wouldn't be that odd if one such plant could cause memory loss and confusion.

Whatever the case, Merry and her group were taken to Alterna and were offered enough money to cover their living expenses for the time being if they became volunteer soldiers. With no idea what was going on, they had accepted this offer in order to survive.

Though they had come at a different time, Haruhiro and the others had apparently become volunteer soldiers via a similar course of events.

There were hundreds of volunteer soldiers like them, some percentage of whom had died, had their bodies burned to ash, and been buried beneath the graves scattered across the hill.

"It's kind of incredible, huh?" Kuzaku said with a sigh.

By "incredible" he must have meant "terrible."

Hiyomu had talked about switching sides and becoming the ones who used others. In other words, Haruhiro and everyone else who'd had their memories stolen had been *used* from the beginning. Did that mean that being pushed into becoming volunteer soldiers was part of that use?

Who was the mastermind behind all of this? Higher-ups in the Kingdom of Arabakia? Hiyomu's master? Or someone else pulling the strings in the shadows? If they had obeyed Hiyomu, they might have found out. It was too late for that now.

Besides, Hiyomu had demanded they obey her, not that they become her comrades or help her. She had the upper hand. It wasn't an even trade. It was fair to consider the possibility that she would still have taken advantage of them. Haruhiro wanted to think that made it fine that things had turned out this way, but there were too few positives about the situation for him to feel that was true.

Their group proceeded farther north through the forest. Once they were through the not particularly large woods, there would be an imposing fortress called Deadhead Watching Keep, which was supposed to be guarded by the Kingdom of Arabakia. Alterna had fallen to the enemy, but they had yet to see what had happened to the keep.

When they came out of the forest, they saw a building that certainly looked like a fortress across a barren field. Bushes grew here and there, and lumber and quarried stone were scattered around. But that wasn't all. There were watchtowers dotted everywhere. Each had several tents around it. Some had fences too.

There were people on top of some of the towers and fences. No, not people.

Haruhiro and his group hid behind piles of lumber and stone, surveying the camp from a distance. The figures looked human but clearly were not. They were maybe a little larger than humans.

Their hair was a bright whitish color, but likely not due to age. Their skin was probably green.

"Orcs..." Merry said.

Unfortunately, Haruhiro didn't remember this, but Deadhead Watching Keep had once been occupied by orcs. The Kingdom of Arabakia's Frontier Army and volunteer soldiers had attacked and retaken it. Incredibly, Haruhiro and his party had taken part in the battle, and they had actually made a major contribution.

At the time, Kuzaku had been in another party. He'd had other comrades. However, Kuzaku had lost them all in that battle. One of Haruhiro's comrades had died in that battle as well. He didn't remember it at all, but it apparently happened.

They had won. The volunteer soldiers received a large amount of money as a reward. It had cost Haruhiro's party a lot of pain to get it, though.

In any case, the Kingdom of Arabakia had regained Deadhead Watching Keep. Did the all these orcs mean it had been taken back?

"Alterna was occupied by the enemy, so this shouldn't come as a surprise." Setora was as calm as ever. "Did the Kingdom of Alterna have any bases other than Alterna and that fortress?"

"We should've taken that map from the second floor of the Forbidden Tower." Merry started drawing a map on the ground. "If this is Alterna..."

North of Alterna was a vast plain called the Quickwind Plains. Southwest of the Quickwind Plains, about thirty kilometers west-northwest from Alterna, the Kingdom of Arabakia's Frontier Army had a garrison at the Lonesome Field Outpost.

On top of that, another ten kilometers or so west of the Lonesome Field Outpost, along the Jet River, stood Riverside Iron Fortress, which was also a base for the Frontier Army. This fortress, like Deadhead Watching Keep, had once been under or-cish control. The Frontier Army had taken Riverside Iron Fortress at the same time as Deadhead Watching Keep.

"I don't want to be too pessimistic, but..." When Kuzaku had such a gloomy look on his face, you couldn't help but feel the situation was really bad. "It's hard to be super optimistic about this...outpost? At Lonesome Field, or this whatever-it-was at Riverside."

"He has a point," Setora said in a flat tone. "Though it's not impossible that the soldiers who fled from Deadhead Watching Keep have gathered at Riverside Iron Fortress and are holed up there, they'll likely be under siege if they are."

"Is there anywhere else we can go?" Shihoru looked so gloomy that she seemed like she might just up and die at any moment. "Anywhere...at all...?"

Merry pointed to a spot on her crude map about a meter up and to the right of Alterna. "If we go back to Vele, we'll be safe for a time. The Free City of Vele is neutral. Humans, orcs, undead, and goblins all live there."

"That's pretty far, huh?" Haruhiro asked.

Merry nodded. "I couldn't tell you the exact distance, but it's probably around five hundred kilometers..."

"Well..." Kuzaku put on a strained smile. "That's, what? A twenty-day walk...?"

"With no guarantee of food?" Setora looked at Kuzaku with exasperation. "If your goal is to die along the way, that might not be a bad idea."

"You're being a little spiteful, aren't you, Setora-san?"

"That wasn't my intent at all. I do think the things you say are beyond foolish, though."

Haruhiro nearly let out a sigh, but without realizing it, he held it in.

Yeesh. It feels like we're blocked in on all sides. He wanted to say that. But this wasn't a situation where he could just throw up his hands. Even though, honestly, he was feeling depressed, Haruhiro didn't let it show on his face. That wasn't because he was determined not to. He just didn't for some reason.

"I want more information," Haruhiro said, desperate, but doing his best to maintain a level tone. "Precise information. That, along with water, and something to eat, I guess. It'd be good if we could hunt."

"If only Yume were here..." Merry said, then shook her head. "Not that saying that's going to help."

"Yume?" Shihoru asked.

"Our comrade," Merry said with a slight smile. When she recalled this Yume person, she couldn't help but grin. That kind of smile. "Yume ended up separating from the group for a little while. We were supposed to meet back up in Alterna half a year after that, but...who even knows how much time has passed since then?"

Shihoru pressed both hands against her chest. "Yume..."

"Did you remember something?" Haruhiro asked.

Shihoru lowered her eyes and shook her head. "That's...not it. It's just... I don't know why, but...it hurts, for some reason..."

"You and Yume were really close," Merry said with a smile. "Yume's a hunter, and just a great kid. I mean that. Strong, earnest, and funny."

Kuzaku whispered in Haruhiro's ear. "She's a girl, right? This Yume-san."

"Probably," Haruhiro replied quietly.

"Me and Haruhiro are the only guys?" Kuzaku counted on his fingers. "Isn't the number of girls kinda high?"

"Man..."

"No, I mean, come on." Kuzaku said weakly. He had to be curious about what the romance situation had been like. When there was a group with guys and girls, that sort of stuff came up naturally, or it was natural for it to come up, or something like that.

Haruhiro could only smile wryly. He wasn't completely un-interested himself, but...he didn't know how to praise a woman's appearance. In terms of words, he would probably call them "pretty," or "cute," but what kind of person was pretty, and what kind was cute? In his estimation, Merry would definitely fall under "pretty." Setora leaned toward "pretty," too. What about Shihoru? "Cute," maybe? But in Shihoru's case, he couldn't deny the womanly aspects of her appearance left a stronger impression. Regardless, all three of them were what you might call attractive in their own ways.

Thinking about it again, Haruhiro had to cock his head to the side a bit and wonder at how he was able to interact with them so normally. If he were tall and muscular like Kuzaku, he might have an easy time attracting the opposite sex, but he wasn't. Just as he started to think about how he was plain, mediocre—no, even less than that—Haruhiro touched his own face. Suddenly, he snapped to his senses.

Though he hadn't looked in the mirror to check what it looked like, Haruhiro was able to imagine his own face. Like he'd suspected, he remembered more than just his name. Not that remembering his own boring face made him terribly happy or anything.

"Anyway, we're not safe here, so let's move away from the fortress," he said. "We can talk about what to do next later." He was talking almost like a leader. Feeling embarrassed, he added, "That okay?"

It seemed no one had any objections.

Haruhiro went back into the forest. First, he wanted to secure a place where they could rest. This forest was too close to both Alterna and Deadhead Watching Keep. They probably needed to go somewhere else. Haruhiro had planned to talk it over, but apparently his thinking had been too naive.

As soon as they went back into the forest, Kiichi looked one way, then suddenly stood up and looked the other. He seemed awfully tense. Not long afterwards, they heard the barking of dogs. That settled it.

"That's probably the goblins coming after us..."

"The question is how big their party is." Setora was still calm. "If it's ten, or even twenty, we can send them packing. But if it's a hundred, maybe two, then that's clearly more than we can handle, don't you think?"

"Nah." Kuzaku tried to act tough for a moment, but then he admitted she was right. "Okay, I've gotta agree."

"Is it just goblins?" Shihoru asked hesitantly. "The goblins and orcs are allies, aren't they...?"

Merry lowered her eyes. "I don't know the exact relationship between goblins and orcs, but they both definitely belong to the Alliance of Kings."

There was no denying the possibility that the goblins of Alterna might have sent a messenger to the orcs of Deadhead Watching Keep, and that they were now searching for Haruhiro and the others together.

Kuzaku groaned. "Orcs look tough, huh? They're big."

For the moment, the goblins and orcs had yet to find their group. But once they did, it was going to be a pretty rough situation.

"There's Damuro to the west. The Cyrene Mines are north-west of there..." Merry shook her head. "Damuro is the goblin base, and the Cyrene Mines are full of kobolds..."

"What's to the east?" Setora asked.

Merry thought for a moment before answering. "If we head east from these woods, we should come out onto the Quickwind Plains. Beyond that, I wouldn't expect to find any towns, at least."

"The south is..." Haruhiro looked southward. "Mountains, huh? A whole mountain range. How about we go into the mountains?"

Merry shook her head. "I wouldn't recommend it. There are dragons in the Tenryu Mountain Range... You know what dragons are, right?"

When he heard the word, every hair on Haruhiro's body stood on end. "I've got a sense."

"Hold on. Dragons?" Kuzaku frowned. "That sounds dangerous."

Shihoru's shoulders slumped. "There's nowhere we can go..."

"Let's head east," Haruhiro said, but immediately thought, *Is that really okay?* and started to get cold feet. Besides, was it really his place to decide? He wasn't up to the task, was he? He didn't even have his memories. No matter how you looked at it, this was beyond him.

But he hadn't just said that at random. He did have some reasoning. "I'm not suggesting we just keep on heading east. I think we should shake off our pursuers first. East is our best option for that, isn't it?"

Setora nodded. "Then let us make haste."

The group set off at once. Haruhiro didn't know if everyone was fully convinced. But if they dawdled, their pursuers might catch them.

The group moved quickly, not stopping to rest at all. Despite that, they still heard the barking of dogs, which wasn't quite coming from ahead but wasn't straight behind them either. Their pursuers were scattered throughout the forest. They had likely formed teams of one dog and one goblin, and there were ten teams, or perhaps even tens of teams, combing the forest to find them.

The group walked and walked. None of them wasted breath chatting. Merry had said this forest wasn't that big, but they still weren't out of the trees by the time the sun was going down. Haruhiro felt like they had walked more than ten kilometers. It had probably been fifteen kilometers, or maybe even twenty.

The area around them was dark, and the western sky burned red. When Haruhiro stopped and turned to look back, everyone stopped. He listened closely. He heard nothing but the tweeting of birds and the rustling of leaves.

Kuzaku opened his mouth for the first time in a while. "When do you think was the last time you heard a dog?"

"Quite some time ago." Setora answered.

Shihoru's shoulders were heaving. She looked pretty badly spent.

It grew darker by the moment as they talked. The sun would soon sink below the horizon.

"Let's rest here for today," Haruhiro suggested, then smiled at Shihoru.

Shihoru gave him a slightly awkward smile in return.

In terms of setting up camp, all they could do was look for a place where they could lie down. They could make impromptu beds out of leaves and grass, but since they were being pursued, Haruhiro didn't want to leave any obvious signs they had been here.

Though sunset was approaching, it was still a little bright. They all sat down in a circle.

"Huh? Where's Kiichi?" Kuzaku asked.

"He just took off somewhere." Setora sounded unconcerned. "He'll come back eventually, I assume."

"Maybe he'll go get us something," Kuzaku said with a laugh.

Setora shrugged. "I'm so blessed."

After that, they all fell silent. Obviously, everyone had to be exhausted after what they'd been through. It was too much effort to search for something to talk about.

Once it was dark enough that you couldn't see more than a few meters away, the women went off into the bushes to go take care of business. Once they came back, Haruhiro and Kuzaku went somewhere a little further away to go take a piss themselves.

"You think we pissed standing side by side like this before we lost our memories, Haruhiro?"

"Who knows? I don't."

"Ah! You just thought I'm the kind of guy who says stupid stuff, didn't you?"

"Maybe a bit, yeah."

"But this kind of stuff could trigger a memory, you know?"

"Did you remember something?"

"Not at all."

When they went back to their campsite, there was a pair of gleaming eyes next to Setora. "Nyaa." Kiichi welcomed them with a meow.

"It seems I truly am blessed." Setora's voice was uncharacteristically cheerful. "Kiichi brought berries. Not many, but enough to tide us over."

Kuzaku jumped in surprise. "Seriously?!"

"He's a clever little guy, huh?" Haruhiro said, and Kiichi gave a short meow in response.

Setora offered Haruhiro something, so he took it. It was one of those berries, apparently. He couldn't tell what color they were in the darkness, but they were about the size of the tip of his thumb, and round. The skin of the fruit had an elasticity.

"It's probably not poisonous," Setora said, so Haruhiro put the berry in his mouth. He bit into it, breaking the skin, and the moisture spread throughout his mouth along with a sour taste. It was a little sweet too.

Kuzaku took one of the berries and ate it. "I feel alive again..."

"That's an exaggeration," Setora said with a snort.

This wasn't going to be enough to satisfy their empty stomachs, and though it had assuaged their thirst, that would also return in no time. Still, Haruhiro could understand how Kuzaku felt. He was relieved as well.

He felt like he could go to sleep right away, but thought, *That's not what I should be doing right now,* and reconsidered. "I'll stand watch. The rest of you, sleep."

"All by yourself?" Shihoru asked.

"Yeah. Does that make you uneasy? Me doing it alone. Yeah. I guess it would, huh?"

"Th-that's not it..."

"You need to sleep, too," Setora said in exasperation. "We can take shifts on watch. It would be a nuisance if you were to collapse from exhaustion."

"You could have worded that better," Kuzaku said.

"Did you want to complain about something?" Setora asked.

"You don't have to get so scary about every little thing..."

"Coward. You frighten too easily."

Ultimately, they decided that they would sleep in shifts while they waited for dawn.

"Well, I'll take the first shift, then. I'll wake up Kuzaku before I hit my limit."

"'Kay." Kuzaku said, then immediately lay down and let out a yawn. "Yikes. I feel like I could fall asleep instantly..."

"Not me..." Shihoru said, so Haruhiro opted to have her stay awake with him.

Merry and Setora lay down too. Kiichi curled up next to Setora. It wasn't long before Kuzaku was lightly snoring. Merry and Setora didn't stir at all. Were they already asleep? Or just trying to get to sleep?

Haruhiro looked around the area, but the forest was locked in a darkness so deep it felt suffocating. It was surprising how little he could see. An owl, or something like it, hooted. As for that chirping sound, was it some sort of insect, maybe?

"It's kind of scary, huh?" Shihoru said in a quiet voice.

Haruhiro, weirdly enough, was not frightened, but he agreed with her. "Yeah."

Shihoru huddled close to Haruhiro's right side. He couldn't see her, but he could sort of tell. It seemed she was trembling.

"You okay?" Haruhiro asked.

"Yeah." She didn't sound okay, but that was probably the only answer she could give. Even if she said she wasn't okay, Haruhiro couldn't do anything about it. It would be nice if there was some sign of things getting brighter, but the future was as dark as the area around them. "Sorry," Shihoru added.

It must be bothering her, Haruhiro thought, but all he could do was ask, "What?" He hated how powerless that made him feel.

"I'm just holding everyone back..."

"No—" Haruhiro started to say, but even if he told her she wasn't, Shihoru wasn't going to be able to accept it.

"If only..." Shihoru was having trouble forcing the words out. "I could remember...how to use magic..."

Haruhiro kept rubbing his nose, touching his lips, and scratching his forehead. Finally, he opened his mouth. "You shouldn't rush it."

"Yeah, you're right. Even if I do try to rush, I've forgotten it...." There was a whine in Shihoru's voice.

Honestly, Haruhiro thought, *Talking to me about it isn't going to help,* but maybe that was cold. Shihoru was his comrade, even if he had forgotten her. He shouldn't have been thinking that way.

Haruhiro wanted to reassure Shihoru, if he could. But how? He couldn't think of anything, and he honestly didn't believe he had the words. That irritated him. He was doing his best to hide that irritation, at least.

Shihoru hugged her knees, grabbing the grass with her left

hand, then letting go of it again. Shihoru wanted to do something, too, but she couldn't, and that must have been frustrating for her.

It was probably by accident, or at least Haruhiro thought so, but Shihoru's left hand touched Haruhiro's right thigh.

"S-sorry!" Shihoru yanked her hand back, and she might have been trying to stand up, but something went wrong, and she ended up falling to the ground. "Urgh…"

"Sh-Shihoru…?"

"I-I can't take this anymore…" Shihoru said in a vanishingly small voice.

She was crying. It seemed like she'd tried to stifle it but failed. It was at least obvious to Haruhiro, who was right next to her. Shihoru was sobbing.

He couldn't leave her alone, but he had no idea what he could do for her. Haruhiro agonized and agonized until, finally, he reached out with his hand. When his fingers brushed up against something soft, he suspected, just maybe, he had touched a spot he absolutely should not touch.

No, that wasn't it. Judging by their relative positions, her demeanor, and more, this was Shihoru's arm. It was definitely not her breasts, for instance. He was almost certain this was her left arm. But even if it was her arm, she might be upset that he'd touched her so suddenly. Haruhiro regretted it. He shouldn't have done it, but it was too late. He couldn't take it back now.

Shihoru stiffened for a moment, but she didn't try to brush his hand away. It was too early to assume that meant there was

no problem, though. He needed to observe some restraint, at the very least.

Doing his best not to grab her too hard, he grasped Shihoru's arm as gently as he could. "I don't think it'll get any worse."

Couldn't he come up with something better than that? Haruhiro couldn't help but despair at his utter lack of linguistic ability. But despite that, Shihoru nodded. She must have felt sorry for him. Here she was, crying, and yet he went and made her feel sorry for him. He felt terrible about that.

Had Haruhiro been better than this before he lost his memories? Whether he had or not, he hoped from the bottom of his heart that he could become a little better in the future.

5 | Give Us Blessings

HARUHIRO STARTED MOVING AGAIN before the sun rose. There was no sign of their pursuers closing in, and more than that, they needed water, as well as food.

Kiichi was their key to both. The nyaa was cat-like, but he walked on his hind legs like a monkey. His front legs were quite dexterous. According to Merry, nyaas were highly intelligent animals. He even seemed to understand his master Setora's words.

The group headed toward the mountains in the south. It was dangerous to climb the mountains because there were dragons, but they might still be safe in the foothills, and they could run away if things got dicey. It would be easier to find a water source in the mountains than the plains.

"Listen," Setora explained to Kiichi that they were looking for food and water. "Without food and water, we will die. So will you. Food and water. Got it?"

By the time the sun had risen high in the sky, the number of steep slopes had increased. There was some mountain-y, mountainous, mountain-like scenery. Maybe it was time to turn back. If a dragon showed up, they were going to be in trouble. Haruhiro and the others decided not to press any further south.

That's when Kiichi took off running. They followed him and eventually came to a valley, at the bottom of which was a thin river. The nyaa dipped his nose into the water and began drinking.

Setora was delighted. "Well done, Kiichi!"

It wasn't a good idea to drink raw water. Even without their memories, they had retained that much common sense, but the group was ridiculously parched. They couldn't resist gulping down some of that clear, ice-cold water.

"We've been living a pretty harsh lifestyle." There was a slight sparkle in Merry's eyes once she had sufficiently rehydrated herself. "I don't think our stomachs will upset too easily. So long as we have water, we should survive for a while."

Just what kind of life had they been leading? Haruhiro was going to have to get the details on that from Merry. He also decided to have Merry explain what she knew about Shihoru's magic. For the time being, they would base themselves out of this watering hole until they got set up. Whatever they ultimately decided to do, they needed to build a solid foundation for surviving first.

The night before, Haruhiro had failed to cheer up Shihoru when she felt crushed by the weight of uneasiness and responsibility. He'd thought about it, but Haruhiro was just as uneasy, and he didn't have the emotional leeway to handle it. He didn't know what he could do, and he worried he couldn't do anything at all. The fact was, he *hadn't* been able to do anything. He hadn't even tried to, so that was obvious.

He wanted to increase the number of things they did, and that they could do, little by little. Even if they couldn't get their memories back, they were fortunate enough to have Merry. They could take in the information she had, bit by bit, and make it their own. They also had Kiichi. Setora's pet nyaa wasn't just good for finding food and water; it seemed he could do much more. He was way more useful than Haruhiro.

It was important to rely on the others, too, not just Kiichi. There was an upper limit to what Haruhiro could accomplish himself. Even if there was something he couldn't do, one of the others might be able to do it. There were probably things that some of the others were unable to do that he could. Besides, even if he wasn't able to do something alone, if two or three of them worked together, they might be able to accomplish it.

It was hard to tell if plants were poisonous or not, but they took the things that Kiichi could eat and tried pressing them to their lips, or putting them in their mouths, and carefully checked that nothing strange happened.

There were multiple nuts and berries, and surprisingly also a moss that was relatively tasty and decently filling. Kuzaku got a stomachache when they experimented with mushrooms and tubers, so they avoided them after that.

Kiichi could capture small animals too: mice, lizards, snakes, and the like. The mice and lizards were too small, so they only amounted to snacks for Kiichi. The snakes were bony, but not inedible.

When it came to the matter of whether to make a fire, they discussed it as a group and considered the question carefully. If they made a cooking fire, it was guaranteed to produce smoke. On a clear day with no wind, that smoke could likely be seen from several kilometers away. But having a fire would make a big difference. Many things could be eaten safely when cooked.

They built a stone oven in a closed space where even if the smoke did rise, the leaves and trees would block it. Once the oven was ready, they prepared dry leaves and wood, then tried to start a fire. Kuzaku seemed confident, saying, "This'll be a piece of cake," but it was more difficult than he imagined.

They were ready to give up by the time the sun started going down, but Shihoru demonstrated a frightening degree of focus. She rubbed a stick between her hands to rotate it, and she finally succeeded in starting the fire.

The way that Shihoru, who had been convinced of her own uselessness, had worked so hard warmed Haruhiro's heart. He called out to her and said, "You did it."

But Shihoru just acted a little embarrassed, saying, "Now I'm all sweaty," and hung her head.

Though most of their first day surviving in that valley in the foothills was spent building a fire, they began hunting on the second day. But on days two and three, the few small animals Kiichi caught was all anyone was able to bring back.

On the fourth day, Haruhiro threw one of his daggers and

managed to injure a deer. He followed it when it fled and managed to catch it once it was weakened. It was still just a fawn. He finished it off quickly, drained the blood, skinned it, and butchered it. From then on, he was occasionally blessed with prey.

But in the afternoon of the group's seventh day camping in the valley, as Haruhiro was looking idly toward the Tenryu Mountains, he saw a large creature moving around. More than half of the creature's body was above the mountain slope's treetops, so it was probably no exaggeration to say that the thing was massive. It seemed crazy that he could see it at all when he was kilometers away like this.

"That's a dragon?" Setora blinked repeatedly. Her expression didn't change, but she seemed surprised in her own way. "It's huge."

The dragon was cutting across the mountainside. It didn't seem to be descending or climbing, but it wasn't going away either. Looking a bit more closely, Haruhiro could see what seemed to be other dragons farther away.

Dragons lived in the Tenryu Mountains. Merry had heard that soon after becoming a volunteer soldier and had never really doubted it, but this was the first time she had actually seen them for herself.

Dragons really did live in the Tenryu Mountains. They weren't even rare. In fact, they were commonplace. That realization made camping out in the valley scarier, but if anything that big approached them, they'd surely notice it. There was no need for undue fear.

On their tenth day in the valley, the group slowly worked on making ropes with bark and ivy. Using that and some wood, they built a simple shelter. It had no walls deserving of the name, and it was really just pillars with a roof, but it would keep them out of the sun and rain.

They naturally fell into a system where three of them would go hunting and gathering while the other two stayed in the valley to watch the fire, prepare food, and work on reinforcing their little hut.

Setora worked with clay and fired it to make earthenware. It was hard to make bottles with a narrow mouth, but if they had deep jars, they could use them to store food. It was also Setora who suggested they could make waterskins using the stomachs and bladders of the animals they hunted. She washed them well, kneaded them to make them softer, and then inflated them and left them to dry. It was a fairly complex process, but the result at least resembled a waterskin, so now they could carry water with them.

Setora would also have liked to put the hides to good use, but that proved surprisingly difficult. Haruhiro's thief gear had included a needle, but no thread. Without a sturdy string, it was impossible to sew them together, so for now they were just hanging the hides or laying them down wherever. Though, knowing Setora, she was bound to find a way to produce string at some point.

On the seventeenth night, Kuzaku and Setora were on guard. Merry and Shihoru were in the hut, or rather under the roof, and Haruhiro was lying on the ground a little further away.

Haruhiro woke before Kuzaku tried to rouse him. He didn't

think that was because he hadn't been deeply asleep; it was just that he had learned to wake quickly when something happened. "What's up?"

"I dunno. There's this noise—or a presence, you could say. Kiichi noticed it."

"Got it. Just to be safe, go wake Merry and Shihoru."

"'Kay."

Haruhiro headed over to where Setora was crouching next to the stove. In order to keep the fire inside from getting too strong, they would only feed it the bare minimum of kindling that it needed to keep going at night.

Kiichi was beside Setora, glaring into the darkness, tensed to leap into action.

"Is it an animal?" Haruhiro asked.

Setora shook her head. "I don't know. But Kiichi's acting strange."

All that Haruhiro knew was that Kiichi was wary of something. But if Setora said he was acting weird, he must have been. The nyaa was staring ahead and to the left.

"Over there, huh? I'll go take a look."

"Be careful."

"Sure."

Haruhiro moved forward with silent steps, melding into the darkness. In the time he'd spent hunting, a good portion of his instincts as a thief seemed to have come back to him. Even in the nearly pitch-black of night, Haruhiro could move about without making a sound.

He didn't have night vision, so he couldn't see. However, the darkness enhanced and sharpened his other senses, and even the slightest light gave him major clues to work with.

Haruhiro left the valley and advanced about sixty paces before coming to a stop. He heard something like, "Nggh... Ahh... Uhh..."

Was that a voice?

He heard a sound like walking, or more like something being dragged. It was off to the right a bit.

The moonlight streaming down through the gaps in the trees illuminated the moving object faintly. It might have been human. Or someone from a humanoid race. His first thought was, *Are they injured?* Were they wandering around wounded?

Whoever it was came to a stop. Haruhiro couldn't see them, but he felt like they were looking in his direction.

Haruhiro stopped breathing for a moment. His heart was racing. He took a deep breath, trying to calm himself. Had they noticed him? He couldn't say at that point.

Haruhiro put a hand on the hilt of his dagger. Drawing it in complete silence was incredibly difficult. He'd draw when his target moved. Until then, he'd wait. Haruhiro was apparently patient. He could wait as long as he had to.

The target moved. Haruhiro pulled his dagger and fell into a defensive posture.

They weren't coming toward him. They were moving away. Haruhiro hesitated a moment, but he decided to tail them. He didn't mean to pursue too far. He just wanted to know who exactly they were.

Not long after he began chasing, he broke into a cold sweat.

This could be bad... There's something behind me too. Could it be my comrades? he thought. *No. That's not it.*

Kuzaku and the others might have worried for him, but now was not the time for them to come help. They'd actually be in the way if they did. They had to know that much, at least.

Besides, this is similar to the other one.

"Ughh... Ohh... Uhh..."

It had the same sort of—it was probably a voice—as the other one. The same walk too. The sounds of its footsteps were similar.

There were also a number of others, though he wasn't sure if he could call them that. Anyway, whatever they were, this one wasn't alone. There were several of them.

Spending a long time agonizing over what to do was the worst possible option. Haruhiro made a decision. He was going to break off pursuit. He didn't need to go directly back to the valley; he could wander a little and still make it. He just had to calm down, not rush things, and walk.

But as he walked, he lost his calm.

"Ohh..."

"Uhh..."

"Ahh... Ohh..."

"Ohh... Ughh..."

He heard voices from here and there. Not just two or three. There were ten, maybe. Perhaps even more.

At the moment, he didn't think any of them were super close— that was to say, five or six meters in any given direction—but he wouldn't have been surprised if one or two were within ten meters of him.

To his right, he caught a glimpse of a shadow moving. It was weird to call it a shadow when things were so dark, but what he saw was just a shadowy outline. It was humanoid. There was no doubt about that.

There was a downward slope ahead. The valley, huh? He'd made it. He could see the fire. The stove.

"Ahh..."

"Ohh..."

"Uhhh..."

"Ahhhh..."

The voices were getting closer. Were they chasing Haruhiro? If they were, he wasn't feeling much pressure, and they didn't seem to be trying to put it on him. What was this? It was very odd.

Haruhiro descended the slope, heading for the stove. His comrades were all around it.

"Something's coming," was all Haruhiro could say.

"Huh? What do you mean by 'something'?" Setora sounded exasperated, and he couldn't really blame her for it.

"Ah!" Kuzaku looked toward the slope that Haruhiro had just come down.

Haruhiro turned too. Something was stumbling down the hill.

Kuzaku drew his sword. "We've gotta take them out, right?!"

"Yeah." Haruhiro shifted his dagger to a backhand grip. "Don't move away from me. Try not to get separated."

"I'll keep all of you alive," said Merry.

He could hear Shihoru breathing tensely.

It's coming. Whatever the hell it is.

The thing dragged one leg behind it. Its body heaved up and down an awful lot as it moved. Was it human? It didn't look like a goblin. It might have been an orc.

Setora pulled a burning piece of firewood from the stove, and thrust it toward whatever it was. "It's human!" she cried.

At the same time, Merry shouted, "Zombie!"

"Doesn't matter what it is!" Kuzaku sprang forward, his sword flashing.

Kuzaku's sword was long and thick. It was single-edged, so you might have called it a large katana. It would have been pretty hard to control it without Kuzaku's height and muscles.

Kuzaku's large katana easily parted the head of the human, or zombie, or whatever it was from its shoulders.

The severed head fell to the ground and rolled next to the stove. It looked like a man's. He was awfully gaunt, and his hair, which had grown wild, was so stiff it was hard to think it was hair.

"Eeek!" Shihoru let out a shriek.

The severed head's eyes and mouth were still moving.

Setora punted the severed head away. "That was beyond disgusting!"

"Scary!" Kuzaku was a brave man, but even he was shuddering. "This is way too scary! Zombies are—"

"There's more coming!" Setora warned.

Were all of those figures zombies? They shambled down the hill toward the bottom of the valley.

Merry jumped forward. "O Light, may Lumiaris's divine protection be upon you." She was going so fast it looked like she was going to tackle the zombies.

Haruhiro chased after her. "Merry?!"

"Dispel!" Merry got up close to the zombies and cast a spell.

This was literally light magic. There was a bright flash and Haruhiro was forced to close his eyes despite himself. "Ugh..." He quickly opened them again and looked around. It took some time before he could see again.

There were two zombies collapsed at Merry's feet. Motionless. Like corpses.

"They're moving corpses, unable to rest in peace because of the No-Life King's curse!" Merry pressed her fingers to her forehead once more, preparing to cast another spell. "O Light, may Lumiaris's divine protection be upon you."

"They're coming in from all directions!" Setora shouted.

It turned into a melee. Setora and Kiichi protected Shihoru, so Kuzaku swung like mad at the zombies that swarmed in while Haruhiro cut off their heads and kicked them away or stomped them, focusing his efforts on rendering them immobile. Zombies struck by Merry's light magic were turned into corpses, or returned to how corpses should be, but those that weren't kept moving until they couldn't anymore.

Maybe the brain was the thing in control, because bodies that lost their heads stopped moving, but their heads were still full of energy. Though the zombies' heads couldn't actually speak, they could still open and close their jaws. Haruhiro nearly got bitten by one of the zombie heads. If he wasn't careful, he'd really be in danger.

Partially because of how dark it was, the battle with the zombies seemed to drag on forever. Just when Haruhiro thought there were no zombies left nearby, he'd hear more moaning from another direction. He'd see zombies shambling down the slope. He'd hear an eerie chattering, and when he looked around, he'd find a zombie head. No matter how many times he crushed a zombie head under his heel, he could never get used to that awful sensation.

Ultimately, no one in the group was able to relax until the sky brightened and they could see for themselves that there were no more zombies in the area.

During the battle, they noticed the zombies included non-human races. However, all the bodies that Merry hadn't hit with light magic were basically chopped to pieces, so it was hard to tell how many were human and how many had been something else.

But seriously, how many zombies had the group taken out? It was hard to get a rough estimate. Honestly, Haruhiro didn't even want to count.

"We..." Shihoru hesitantly looked at the rest of the group. "We have to clean this up?"

"Yeah..." Kuzaku was in an incredible state, bathed in blackened blood and chunks of flesh. "Guess so. We probably should clean this up, huh? I'm not sure I want to sleep here otherwise."

"There's something more important." Setora was strong to be able to say that. Though not to the same degree as Kuzaku, Setora had her fair share of blood splatter and rotten meat on her, but she seemed unfazed. "Were we targeted by the zombies? Or was this raid a product of coincidence?"

Merry must have been exhausted by how much magic she'd used. She was kneeling. "The dead who are dominated by the No-Life King's curse gather in columns and wander aimlessly. I heard that somewhere before, but I don't know when."

"Then it was coincidental." When Setora reached out her arm, Kiichi climbed up onto her shoulder and licked her cheek. "We had bad luck."

Kuzaku hung his head, letting out a sigh. "Just terrible luck..."

Haruhiro didn't sigh. He would have liked to put a positive spin on this, but that was clearly not going to be possible. He was disappointed, and he wanted to complain too. He wanted to cry his eyes out. He wanted to lash out at someone.

Well, no, not really. Not that he *wasn't* disappointed. It was just that he could handle it. Or he wanted to think he could, at least. If he was able to think like that, then it meant his spirit wasn't broken yet.

"I hate to do it, but let's abandon this place." Haruhiro did his best not to sound reluctant as he said that. "It doesn't look like the goblins of Alterna are looking for us anymore, and we have some preserved food. I think we're ready to move on."

6 | Light on the Plains

THE TERRAIN AHEAD WAS DISTINCTIVE. It was a plateau, but not a high one. It was an incredibly broad, low plateau. As they walked through the scattered shrubs and dry, wheat-colored grass, the plateau still looked low. No more than a slight hill. It took them little time to climb up onto it. Beyond, there was a massive pan-like depression.

"This is the place, huh?" Haruhiro mumbled to himself.

None of his comrades said anything.

The group was standing on the rim of the pan. There was a large spring at the bottom, and then two other smaller springs. The area was surrounded by a fence and moat, and there were a number of buildings inside the fence. But the fence was broken in places, and the buildings were falling apart. The scattered debris must have been part of them at one point.

The moat was filled with spring water, and there was an intact bridge over it. It looked like they could cross.

After some time, Setora spoke. "It looks deserted."

"Looks like," was all Haruhiro could say in response.

"No, but, uh, you know?" Kuzaku was obviously forcing himself to sound cheerful. "It doesn't look like there was heavy fighting, right? Maybe the Frontier Army guys ran away before the enemy arrived."

Because their dead bodies would turn into zombies, the absence of corpses wasn't strange, but the way it had fallen to ruin seemed different from the aftermath of an attack. Though most of the buildings were damaged, there weren't any broken weapons lying around or arrows sticking out of them, and there were no bloodstains or any other signs of battle.

"Do you want to go down and check it out?" Merry sounded like she had a hard time saying that.

"Yeah," Haruhiro replied easily, and he started descending the slope. He didn't need to try particularly hard to keep his calm. He'd more or less anticipated this, so he was ready for it.

He turned back, and like he expected, Shihoru seemed fine too. Haruhiro and Shihoru had some things in common. They didn't look at things too optimistically.

Try to imagine a lottery with two-to-one odds. If either of them played it, they assumed they were almost always going to lose. Though logic dictated otherwise, and they knew the odds were one in two, they couldn't help but assume that, if things were really fifty-fifty, the result would be whichever was worse for them. Even with a four-in-five chance of winning, they were sure to lose. If the odds were nine of ten, they'd suspect they'd somehow still miraculously find a way to lose.

Haruhiro and Shihoru were alike in that they didn't want to rely on good fortune or on other people. They were too scared to. That was why they were fine. They figured this was going to happen.

Here was the group's plan:

First, they would head north from the valley in the foothills and enter the Quickwind Plains. According to Merry, if they continued north across the flat plains, they would be able to see a mountain in the west. It was called Mount Grief, and it was supposed to be a den of undead or something. Some seven or eight kilometers south of Mount Grief, the Arabakia Frontier Army had an outpost at Lonesome Field. It was a little hard to imagine it was still intact if Alterna had fallen, but they hadn't confirmed either way yet. There was still a slim possibility of its survival.

In addition to that, if they went to the Lonesome Field Outpost, they could follow the Jet River to reach Riverside Iron Fortress. Even if the Lonesome Field Outpost was a dud, the remnants of the Frontier Army and the volunteer soldiers might have gathered at Riverside Iron Fortress.

If both the outpost and fortress had been taken, that was obviously the worst possible outcome, but at least their situation would be clear. It would mean they had no allies south of the Quickwind Plains. Rather than cling to hope, it was better to learn the true situation and plan their response accordingly.

Haruhiro took a careful look around the Lonesome Field Outpost, or what was left of it. Like he had suspected, there were no bodies and nothing that looked like bloodstains. He suspected the Frontier Army garrison and the volunteer soldiers had pulled back before they were attacked. The enemy arrived after that and took out their frustration on the deserted buildings.

According to Merry, the outpost had once had a little marketplace, which had sold food, toiletries, arms, and equipment. It looked like those supplies had all been carried off during the retreat. Still, there were some small gains.

In the remains of what had apparently been a Frontier Army barracks was some military equipment, including weapons and armor. The group went through it, and some of it wasn't bad. Merry took a warhammer, and Setora took a spear, sword, and dagger. There were backpacks, shoulder bags, and leather waterskins as well, so they decided to take what they needed.

In the market, they were able to find fabric and leather clothes. Most were old and worn, but nobody was going to complain as long as they were still wearable. The group changed out of their clothes and shoes, which were worn out and full of holes. Now that Shihoru finally had a reasonable outfit, she could say goodbye to that old cloak. They were able to collect a bunch of tools, including a hammer, chisel, nails, and even needles. Haruhiro wanted some string, but they couldn't find any.

During the search, Haruhiro kept an eye on things outside the outpost. He worried someone might be surveilling them from a distance. But, for better or for worse, it didn't seem that way.

The group stopped rummaging for supplies at what seemed like a good time, and they headed for Riverside Iron Fortress. The group's morale hadn't fallen. If anything, everyone seemed a little more cheerful.

From the Lonesome Field Outpost, they headed west, west, and then west some more. The Quickwind Plains stretched for hundreds of kilometers, but with the exception of Mount Grief and the Crown Mountain far to the northeast, it was all flat and mind-numbingly vast. There was little variation in the vegetation, so no matter how far you went, it all looked the same.

There were a number of different species of animals spread across the region, but because it was so wide open, you could see a long way, and sounds carried easily. They saw a lot of animals at a distance, but if the group tried to approach them, they would run away. Hunting in the Quickwind Plains would probably require the clever use of traps, or chasing after their prey and cornering it as a group.

By evening, they hit the Jet River. It was a large river with a violent current, like you might expect from the name, and the far shore was so distant that it looked hazy.

The Jet River's source was somewhere in the Tenryu Mountains to the south, and Haruhiro and the others followed it upstream. Some time after the sun went down, Riverside Iron Fortress came into view.

"It looks like someone's home," Setora said. Haruhiro couldn't tell if she was joking.

Riverside Iron Fortress also served as a river port, so it stuck out into the Jet River a little. There were more than ten towers on the walls, and watch fires were lit all over, so they could see how impressive it looked even at night.

Haruhiro had Kuzaku and the others wait while he approached the fortress alone. There were many groves along the riverbank. He was able to approach quite easily, hiding in the trees and bushes until he was about fifty meters from the fortress walls. It was a grassy field from there onward, and if there were guards, he was at high risk of being spotted. There had to be lookouts. He could see silhouettes on top of the wall.

As Haruhiro wondered, *Okay, so what do I do now?* he heard a howl.

Awoooooooooooooooooooooooo!

Wolves, huh? Or dogs. They sounded similar, but if they were dogs, they might be trained. He was pretty sure the noise came from behind him.

As he turned to head back—*Awoooooooooooo!*—he heard the howling again.

Awoooooooooooooooo!

Awooooooooooooooooooooo!

Awooooooooooooooooooooooooooooo!

There was a chain of howls.

They weren't just behind him. He heard them to the east and even from the fortress. Even now, he could hear them howling. It was like they were responding to one another.

Have I been found? Haruhiro thought as he rushed back to his comrades.

When he was right in front of his destination, something lunged at him from the rear. Haruhiro instinctively threw himself to the ground as he drew his dagger. He rolled, then deflected the white blade coming toward him. Deflected, retreated. Deflected.

Though it was dark, he could tell his enemy was not human, but it was bipedal, and it could use a sword. It had a tail too.

It looks like a dog. A dog standing on its hind legs. Merry had talked about them.

"A kobold, huh?" Haruhiro dodged the kobold's thrust, then got behind it. He didn't even have time to think, *Right here,* before he buried his dagger in its back.

The kobold fell. It died almost instantaneously.

"I saw something."

It was some sort of gleaming line. Was it a hallucination? He shook his head. He didn't have time for this.

It wasn't wolves or dogs howling. It was kobolds.

Merry had said the kobolds were based out of the Cyrene Mines, but the goblins from Damuro had been in Alterna. It wasn't that crazy for them to find kobolds in Riverside Iron Fortress. The goblins and kobolds both belonged to the Alliance of Kings. They were enemies of the Kingdom of Arabakia. Haruhiro ran.

Kuzaku and the others were also being attacked by a group of kobolds.

"Haruhiro?!" Setora was using her spear to keep the kobolds at bay. "You got careless! This whole area is enemy territory!"

"Sorry! I was being naive!" Merry held her warhammer at the ready as she protected Shihoru.

"You didn't know, so can we really blame you?!" Kuzaku swung his large katana and cut down one of the kobolds. "Yeah! Come get some!"

"I can't just keep being protected!" Shihoru looked like she was planning something.

Is it that? *Is she going to do that?*

"Come! Dark!"

According to Merry, after a variety of experiences, Shihoru had stepped outside the framework she was taught at a place called the mages' guild and formulated a new magic. Haruhiro didn't remember it, and he didn't know anything about magic whatsoever, but it sounded pretty incredible. In fact, Merry even told them what Shihoru had accomplished was amazingly impressive.

Even when Merry told her, "So be more confident," Shihoru could only muster a weak, half-hearted smile.

Haruhiro could understand how she felt. She was happy, and grateful for the encouragement, but didn't know how to react to being told "You were incredible." What mattered was what she could do now, and some glorious past she couldn't even remember was no consolation for that.

Shihoru had asked Merry everything she could about her magic, and she was experimenting to try and recreate it. It was not going well. Because Shihoru's magic was entirely her own, Merry only knew the surface details. When the only clue she had to give was a name—Dark—Merry had felt bad and given Shihoru an apologetic look.

Despite that, whenever Shihoru had time, she tried envisioning Dark, trying to make him hers. She tried to pull him out from somewhere, to knead the air into his shape, anything and everything that she could.

Shihoru must have been prepared to taste disappointment every time she tried. Haruhiro understood that well. People like Haruhiro and Shihoru weren't strong enough to believe, *It's okay, you can definitely do this.* Instead, they thought, *I know I can't do it, it's impossible, but I will, because I have no choice.*

It had to be really hard on her. If he were Shihoru, he'd have probably given up along the way.

You're doing great, Shihoru. When he put it like that, it might feel like he was looking down at her, but he really did think so. It wasn't the past Shihoru who was amazing, it was the one right here and now.

From some other world, something opened an invisible door in front of Shihoru's open palms and appeared.

It was black. Deep and thick, like the darkness of night. Long, black strings intertwined in a spiral and took on a certain form. Was it a person? It was small enough to fit in Shihoru's hand.

"Go, Dark!" When Shihoru gave the order, Dark instantly shot toward one of the kobolds.

Nnnshoooooooooooo... Was that the sound of Dark flying, or was it his voice? Whatever the case, it sounded like nothing else.

The kobold seemed shocked, and it didn't look like it even

tried to dodge Dark as he slammed into the kobold's chest. Right after, he suddenly changed trajectory. Pulling a tight turn around the first kobold, he collided with another. That kobold let out a yip and tried to get away. But Dark drove straight forward, assailing yet another target.

Haruhiro looked at Shihoru. She was following Dark with her eyes. No, that wasn't it. It was the opposite. Dark moved where Shihoru looked. Shihoru was controlling Dark.

Shihoru used Dark, who stood out, blacker than the dark of night, and made that distinctive *nshoooooooooo*—which was pretty frightening and really grated on the nerves—to terrify the kobolds and make them panic.

"Not bad, Shihoru!" Setora mercilessly impaled one of the kobolds as it ran around in confusion. Then she shouted at Haruhiro, "What are you doing, you dunce?!"

Setora was harsh as ever, but he couldn't really argue. Haruhiro grappled a kobold, slit its throat with his dagger, and then pushed it down. "Kuzaku, Merry!"

"Yeah! Got it!"

"Okay!"

Kuzaku and Merry fiercely attacked the kobolds closest to them. By the time Haruhiro could count to ten, six or seven kobolds were down. The remaining kobolds yipped and barked as they started to run away.

Somewhere, Kiichi meowed.

"Haruhiro!" Setora pointed to the northwest. "That way! It looks like there are no enemies!"

"Let's go, everyone!" Haruhiro sent Shihoru, Merry, and Kuzaku ahead, then brought up the rear himself. "Setora, lead the way! I'm counting on you!"

"Got it!"

He heard the kobolds howling again. Though they'd driven off the earlier group, they couldn't relax just yet.

Haruhiro and the others were running pretty much as fast as they could. The pace was taking a toll on Kuzaku, who was wearing heavy armor, but he was tough, so he could keep it up for a while even if he was winded. Shihoru seemed especially light on her feet. Was that because she'd found a pair of shoes that fit her in the Lonesome Field Outpost? Or maybe she was reenergized by her success at calling Dark?

There didn't seem to be any pursuers nearby, at least. Once he was sure of that, Haruhiro shouted, "Let's rest!" to Setora up front.

Kuzaku crouched immediately. "Whew. That was tough! What the hell? There were enemies! I know I half-expected there to be, but still…"

Haruhiro smiled wryly. "Only half?"

In a situation like this, only Kuzaku would still half-expect things to work out. Haruhiro had been eighty—no, ninety percent sure that Riverside Iron Fortress had fallen to the enemy. That was why he wasn't dispirited. Haruhiro was already thinking about their next move.

Where in the Quickwind Plains, which were wider than they had any right to be, were they going to head next? There were options.

"To the Wonder Hole?" Shihoru offered hesitantly.

Haruhiro made a point of giving her a big nod. "Yeah."

"That's right." Merry let out a sigh, as if trying to shift her current frame of mind. "The Wonder Hole was a hunting ground for volunteer soldiers. It's complex, and no one knows all the details, but there could still be a volunteer soldier base down there."

"That's a long shot," Setora snorted. "But in this situation, we won't get anywhere by demanding certainty, I suppose. Let's go. Hey."

Even though Setora had just kneed him in the back, Kuzaku didn't even get angry. "All right!" He jumped to his feet. "Let's get going! I rested a bit. We'll just have to go as far as we can. It's not like we can go any farther than that."

"Can't you say anything with a little more substance?"

"Listen, I'm not the guy to look to for advanced tricks like that."

"Is that advanced?"

Haruhiro tuned out their bantering as he looked around. The lights of Riverside Iron Fortress were still visible in the distance. He could hear the kobolds howling, but there was no sign of them getting any closer.

During their stay in the foothills, they had heard about most of the local geography from Merry. The Wonder Hole was northwest of the Lonesome Field Outpost. They would head back to the ruins of the outpost, then head onward from there.

Kiichi suddenly climbed up Setora to perch on her shoulder. Did he want some attention from his keeper? It didn't look like it. Kiichi was staring northward.

"What is it?" Setora looked that way.

"That's..." Haruhiro trailed off. It was faint, but there was something bright, far to the north. Trying not to let his emotions cloud his judgment, he suggested, "A fire, maybe?"

"Hrmm..." Kuzaku groaned and scratched his head.

What were they to make of this? It was hard to say. For now, they decided to proceed toward the light that might be a fire.

When they had walked about a kilometer north, they realized the light was coming toward them too. There was someone carrying a torch or lantern, and they were on the move. Whoever it was, they were probably only a kilometer or so away from the group, though it would be generous to call that even a rough estimate.

"Maybe they're on our side?" Kuzaku said, smiling but not laughing.

Not even Kuzaku honestly thought that whoever it was would be an ally, which was to say, with the Frontier Army or the volunteer soldiers. If the question was if they were friend or foe, yeah, it was probably safe to assume foe.

"Over there." Setora pointed north-northeast, and then again to the east. "Over there too."

It wasn't just one light. They were farther off than the light to the north, but they could see two more. It would be best to assume that wasn't all.

Setora sighed. "Here's hoping they're on foot."

I wonder about that, Haruhiro nearly said, but stopped himself.

Shihoru and Merry were silent.

The dry wind that blew across the Quickwind Plains at night sounded like a low growl. That was a strange sound for wind to make. It sounded a bit similar in tone to someone whistling, too, but Haruhiro couldn't be confident in that description.

Haruhiro felt that, at times like this, he was the kind of person who waited for someone else to make the call on what to do. He wasn't the type to actively decide things. Despite that, according to what Merry told them, Haruhiro had been their leader.

"The north and east seem dangerous," Haruhiro said, even as he thought the position of leader was too heavy for him. "The Jet River and Riverside Iron Fortress are to the west of here, too, so let's go south."

7 | The Present Drifts By Along With the Past

THEY WALKED THROUGH THE NIGHT, and by dawn they had arrived at the forest that spread out at the foot of the Tenryu Mountains.

Though this was still the foothills of the Tenryu Mountains, it was more than fifty kilometers from the group's former campsite—probably more like sixty.

Everyone was completely exhausted, but not knowing the area, it would have been beyond dangerous to just make camp wherever. First they needed to explore, get a grasp on the terrain, find out if there were any dangerous beasts, and check for potential sources of water. The sun had already risen, so they weren't going to have an easy time getting to sleep, anyway. It was best if they got the stuff done that needed doing.

They found a river without much effort. Next to the river was a cave, but it was infested with bats and covered in guano. If they were going to use it, they would have to drive out the bats and clean up their droppings.

The trees here were denser than they had been near the valley. It was like a jungle. Maybe because this was the basin of the Jet River, the trees and plants seemed especially vibrant here. There was a dampness in both the air and the ground.

One time, they caught a glimpse of a large, bipedal lizard-like creature, though only at a distance. Merry said it might be a wild horse-dragon, which was a small species of dragon. Those raised in captivity could apparently carry a person on their back.

In the afternoon, the group rested a short distance from where they first found the river. There were large, mossy rocks, and a small open space in their shadow. A landmark that stood out so much was both a positive and a negative, but they decided to use the rocks as their temporary camping site.

Even as the others sat down on the ground, Haruhiro remained standing. He had a vague feeling that if he sat down now, it would sap his spirit.

Kiichi perched on top of a large boulder, keeping watch. No one spoke. Kuzaku and Merry both tried to say something, but they shut their mouths before uttering a sound.

They had talked a fair amount while searching, and everyone was acting normally, but they had to be feeling despondent. Even if they weren't, it wouldn't be weird for them to feel lost, beaten down, and unmotivated.

Haruhiro had been more or less prepared for this outcome, but the reality was that the Quickwind Plains were occupied by the enemy. They had no allies here—or if they did, they were hiding, just like their own group.

That likely meant there was no allied force large enough to take on the enemies that occupied Alterna, Deadhead Watching Keep, and Riverside Iron Fortress. Even if the Frontier Army and the volunteer soldiers were alive and well, they were in a situation where, like Haruhiro and his group, they'd had to run and hide to survive.

Well, nothing's changed.

Haruhiro was about to say that on several occasions but stopped short every time. Though it was absolutely true, it would not be a particularly effective thing to say.

We have no real hope.

Haruhiro had figured that this area was already full of enemies. He didn't need to say that he didn't believe in the faintest that maybe, just maybe, they had reason to hope.

Honestly, he wanted to cut himself off from hope. He wanted the resolve to accept that they were going to have to survive by themselves. The thought was refreshing to Haruhiro. He didn't even have to fake it or anything.

It was still going to be hard, though. He wanted to shout, *What the hell? Screw this! It's not fair! Just how terrible of a guy was I? Did I do something to deserve this? Even if I did, it's just too cruel!*

But it was only for now. This had to be the worst of it. If he could just trick himself into continuing on, he'd gradually get used to the situation. Actually, he already felt a lot better than yesterday.

He suspected that, even if there was a difference of degree, the whole group felt something similar. Things were rough right now, but if they could just get through these hard times, they'd be able to manage somehow.

"Let's eat," said Haruhiro.

Merry, Setora, and Shihoru looked at Haruhiro as if in a daze. Their responses were dull and weak. Kuzaku didn't even lift his gaze.

Haruhiro whacked Kuzaku upside the head. "Food time."

"Ow!" Kuzaku pressed a hand to his head and looked up at Haruhiro. "Huh? Food?"

"Yeah. Let's eat."

"Yeah, sure."

Even as he thought, *How many times do I have to say it?* Haruhiro repeated himself. "Let's get some food."

Even without heading out to procure more, they still had some food left over from their former camp in the valley. It was just dried meat and berries, but chewing on something would help get their minds going, and they'd be able to relax more when their stomachs weren't empty. They might even be able to chat a little, then.

Out of caution, they decided not to light a fire yet. However, they did discuss where it would be best to put up a roof if they were to build a stove, and where they would sleep.

When it came to these things, the planning stage was always the most fun. Sometimes they got overly excited and came up with unrealistic ideas, but if talking about those dreams helped cheer them up, that was good in its own way.

In the evening, Setora said she was getting sleepy and took a late nap along with Kiichi. Kuzaku lay down, too, and was soon snoring.

As it all happened to work out, in the end it was just Haruhiro, Shihoru, and Merry left awake, sitting around in a triangle an equal distance apart. This was a logical way of sitting, if you wanted to eliminate blind spots. They weren't close, but they weren't too far apart. It felt like a good distance.

But it felt kind of awkward. Why? Haruhiro didn't know. Was he the only one who felt this way? Apparently not, because Shihoru and Merry were both clearly unable to relax. They weren't chatty by nature, but even considering that, they were being really quiet.

Haruhiro decided to go for it and try to get the conversation rolling. "Dark."

Shihoru nodded. "Yeah."

"You did it. Dark. Magic."

"Yeah." Shihoru nodded once more, then smiled. "I did it."

The corners of Haruhiro's lips turned up a little too. He would've had a hard time really smiling. Actually, he couldn't have. "I'm happy for you. Really. It's great."

"Yeah...I'm glad."

"Your control was perfect too. Control... Is that the right word? It's not weird, right?"

"It's not...weird. I think it fits."

"Oh, yeah? That's good." Haruhiro rubbed his cheek. "Is that overstating it? Saying it's good."

Shiboru shook her head. "If you say it's good, Haruhiro-kun... That makes me...happy."

Haruhiro nearly said, *Oh, yeah?* again, but he swallowed the words and searched for something else to say, but he failed to come up with anything.

"Yeah," Merry mumbled.

When Haruhiro looked over, Merry's eyes were lowered.

"That's good," she said to no one in particular. Her lips were smiling, but she seemed sad, somehow.

What could it be? Haruhiro found it odd, but he didn't know how to talk to her about it.

Eventually, Setora, Kiichi, and Kuzaku woke up. The sun was setting. They all ate one more time before it got too dark out.

"Can I say something indulgent?" Kuzaku asked while chewing on a piece of dried meat.

"No," Haruhiro said without hesitating.

Kuzaku looked like he was going to cry. "Whaa...?"

"If I don't have to listen, you can say all you want," Setora said, distancing herself from him.

"If you're not gonna listen, what's the point...? I just wanted to say, 'It'd be nice if we could all eat better food together,' that's all."

Haruhiro sighed with an exaggerated shrug of his shoulders. "You said it anyway."

"Aw, come on. You were all just messing with me, right?" Kuzaku looked at them. "Am I wrong? You were messing, right? Like it's obligatory. Huh? You weren't?" He turned and looked away. No one responded. "Huh? Huh?" Kuzaku started to panic. "Was I wrong? Did I misunderstand? Am I annoying, maybe? Do you guys kind of hate me?"

Unable to watch any longer, Shihoru gave him a slight smile. "That's not true."

"I-I know, right?!" Kuzaku seemed exaggeratedly relieved. "Whew, you had me, there! Teaming up on me like that! Don't tell me everyone but me's actually got their memories back already, right?!"

Obviously that wasn't the case, but they were able to communicate like they had been together for years. Not always. But there were times, occasionally, when it felt that way.

"Maybe you don't really need memories," Merry said all of a sudden. "What's important isn't the past, it's now."

What had made Merry say something like that? Unlike Haruhiro and the others, Merry had her memories, which had helped them a lot. He couldn't remember anything, try as he might, so it was a moot point, but Haruhiro had never once thought he didn't *need* his memories.

If Hiyomu or someone else were to show up right now and offer him his stolen memories back unconditionally, he probably wouldn't have refused. He really wanted them back.

Once the thick curtain of night had fallen, the group took turns on watch and sleeping. Kuzaku and Setora had already gotten some shuteye during the evening, so they stood watch with Kiichi, then woke Haruhiro in the latter half of the night.

Merry woke up, too, but Shihoru was sound asleep.

"Why not let her rest a little longer?" Setora said, gesturing to Shihoru with her chin. "Her magic is useful. We need to keep her in a state where she can exert her power if need be."

"You could have worded that better..." Kuzaku said, turning to Haruhiro with a "Right?" as he looked for agreement.

For his part, Haruhiro wanted to let Shihoru rest too. Even if they let her be, this was Shihoru, so he felt like she'd wake up on her own. For now, he decided to go on watch with Merry.

It was only a moment before Kuzaku was out like a light. Setora lay down, cuddling Kiichi, neither tossing nor turning.

Haruhiro tried asking about something that had bothered him. "Hey, Merry."

"What?" Merry responded in a calm tone.

How was he supposed to bring this up? "No, uh... It's fine, forget about it."

Merry chuckled. "Oh, yeah?"

"It's not fine, but..." Haruhiro trailed off. "It's not *not* fine."

"You know, this kind of takes me back."

"Huh?"

"The way you're talking. It's like how you used to, a long time ago."

"How I used to? Oh. You mean before losing my memory?"

"Even before that." Merry sighed. "I'm sorry. With things like this, it might have been better to have no memories at all..."

"No, but you do remember. Isn't it obvious you'd think about how things were before?"

"I'm the only one who knows, though."

"Hrm..." Haruhiro pulled on his bottom lip several times. "But, I dunno, they're important memories for you...aren't they?"

There was a brief pause before Merry responded. "Hmm. Well, yes. They're very important."

"Then I don't think you can say you don't need them. It helps all of us that you remember. The fact is, without your memories, I don't know what would have happened to us."

"But, you know?"

"Yeah?"

"It's just..." Merry lowered her voice. "That's not all there is to it. There're things I'm not telling you."

"There are?"

"Because there are some things I don't think I need to."

Such as? Haruhiro wanted to ask, but he couldn't. If he took it at face value, those "things she didn't need to tell him" meant "things that were of low importance." But was that really the case? It might be that they weren't unimportant, but that there were other reasons she didn't—or couldn't—tell him.

Maybe Merry had her own reasons for not wanting to talk about it. She might have been deliberately keeping those things to herself. Haruhiro was curious enough that he couldn't help wanting to question her about it. Still, despite his curiosity, he didn't want to force her.

"Speaking of the past, I know you said I was the leader, but..." Haruhiro said in a cheerful voice. Or at least, what he tried to present as a cheerful voice. "I just can't believe it. I can't imagine I'm suited for it, in terms of personality."

"You might not have been the type that pulls everyone along," Merry replied casually. "You brought us together in a way that was different from anyone else, a way only you could."

"Huh? What was that like? Was I so unreliable that everyone else worked harder or something?"

"I've never once thought you were unreliable," Merry said. "Oh, but don't misunderstand," she added. "I'm not telling you what you should do now, or how I want you to be, Haru."

Merry was being very considerate toward Haruhiro. Why was she being so nice? Because they were comrades, of course.

But it's "Haru," huh? Haruhiro thought. Merry was the only one who called him that.

Haruhiro was a bit long, so if everyone called him Haru, there would be nothing noteworthy about it. But that *wasn't* the case. Everyone but Merry called him Haruhiro, or Haruhiro-kun. Maybe it was just that Haru was easier to say. Kuzaku, Setora, and Shihoru were all three syllables, while Haruhiro was four, so Merry shortened it. That might have been all there was to it.

"You have a way of taking things at your own pace. You might not look like it, but you're stubborn. In a good way."

"Is there a good way to be stubborn...?"

"When you're doing something, isn't it important to have some part of you that doesn't waver? Without that, you'll be pulled every which way."

"Ohh, I get it."

"I was fixated on the past. I still am now, though..." Merry said. Then, in a quieter voice, "Maybe that's my personality," she added.

"On the past," Haruhiro parroted.

"I could never face forward. You—everyone saved me."

"I can't imagine I was much of a forward-thinking person myself." He wasn't just trying to hide how he was embarrassed by her praise; he really did think that. Haruhiro didn't have the cheer that kept Kuzaku from ruminating on things, or the rational mind that let Setora think clearly and avoid negativity.

"Well..." Merry thought for a moment. "Maybe you weren't forward-thinking. It's not that you planned all the next steps ahead before making your move. More like you never took your eye off what was in front of you in the moment."

"Hrm... So, I was steady?"

"If I had to put a word to it, maybe that's it?"

"If you told me I was careful, or cautious, or something like that, I'd sort of understand..."

"At the same time, you could be bold too."

"Huh? I could?"

"Sometimes, sure," Merry said with a mischievous smile. "You surprised me a number of times. But any time you did something that surprised me, it was never for you. It was for your comrades. That's why I...why I felt the way I did about you."

"Why you felt the way you did...?" Haruhiro echoed.

"I could never thank you enough for what you did for me."

"Naw..." was all Haruhiro could say. He didn't remember doing anything that merited gratitude. He literally did not remember.

"Sorry," Merry apologized. "Oh, gosh. What am I doing? Here

I am, fixating on the past again. Even though it doesn't mean a thing to the rest of you."

Haruhiro shook his head. He didn't think it was meaningless. But while Merry remembered everything, Haruhiro couldn't recall a thing about it. Maybe he and Merry had shared some memories. It was possible they had been important to both of them. But Haruhiro didn't remember, and he couldn't seem to call those memories back.

Basically, what Merry was saying was that even if a memory was meaningful to her, it had no meaning for Haruhiro, and so could not realistically be meaningful to him. That gulf between them frustrated her.

On Haruhiro's end, if anything, he wanted to apologize for forgetting. That would just trouble Merry, though, so he obviously wasn't going to.

"Um..." Shihoru spoke.

"Ah!" Merry panicked. "Sh-Shihoru, you were awake? S-since when?"

"Erm... For a while?"

"Were you listening?"

"J-just a little..."

"O-oh... I see. So you were listening... You could have said something."

Haruhiro put on a vague smile and said, "Yeah." What was Merry so flustered about? It made no sense to him.

Shihoru got up and crawled over to where they were. Maybe she couldn't see, because she ran into Haruhiro. "Eek...!"

"Oh! A-are you okay?"

"I-I'm fine..." Shihoru said as she sat down next to Haruhiro.

He felt like she was a bit close, but that was probably because it was hard to judge distance in the darkness.

"I'm sorry. I..." Shihoru bowed her head so deeply he could tell even without being able to see her. "I overslept. You must have tried to wake me up, but I didn't... Right...?"

"Nah, we never tried to wake you up," Haruhiro responded.

"Huh...? You didn't? Why not...?"

"You were sleeping so well that we started talking about just letting you rest. So we did."

"Yeah," Merry agreed. "You must have been exhausted..."

Shihoru was silent. Had they hurt her feelings? She might have felt wounded that they were giving her special treatment, or that she wasn't being seen as an equal.

"We should have woken you up, huh?" Haruhiro tried saying. "We didn't mean anything bad by it..."

Shihoru shook her head vigorously. "I never thought that you did... I'm sorry."

Why was she apologizing? Well, it wasn't that Haruhiro didn't understand. Shihoru was a serious person. She had a low opinion of herself, so she felt emotionally cornered, thinking that she needed to try harder than everyone else.

He wanted to tell her she could take it easy, but even if he did, Shihoru probably wouldn't be able to relax. All that Haruhiro could do was respect her wishes and be ready to support her when the time came. He needed to pay close attention so that he could reach out to her if she looked like she was about to break—no, before it got to that point.

Haruhiro raised his right hand and reached out to touch Shihoru's back.

Whoa, there, he thought, and pulled his hand back. *What am I doing? No, I didn't do it. It was a failed attempt. Thank goodness. It was only an attempt.*

She was a girl. He couldn't just touch her like that. It would be immoral, or inappropriate. Anyway, he couldn't. He just always found himself wanting to cheer Shihoru on. Obviously, he didn't have any ulterior motives for it. Or so he thought.

Hmm, did he? Haruhiro couldn't say that he didn't have the want, the desire to touch women. He might have, a little. Could he say for sure that this wasn't a manifestation of that?

Once he started thinking about that, he couldn't say a word. First Shihoru got all quiet, and now Haruhiro was silent too. From Merry's perspective, this probably wasn't a situation where she could say anything.

The three of them watched the area as they waited for dawn. Their hearts were certainly not at ease. Haruhiro's wasn't, at least. But on the surface, all was quiet.

8 | Rusty Eyes

THEIR CAMP IN THE SHADOW of the rocks grew more complete by the day. Now that they had tried living here, Haruhiro could tell the surrounding area held a greater bounty than what they'd had access to in the valley. There was a greater variety of plants, and not just edible ones, but an abundance of sturdy vines as well.

Some ivy they found could be used as rope, obviously, but Setora also experimented with it and found it worked as a bowstring too. Setora would have had trouble making arrows with proper arrowheads, but the penetrating power of even a plain pointy stick was not to be underestimated. Having bows made a huge difference in how efficiently they were able to hunt.

They had gotten nails at the Lonesome Field Outpost, plus they had access to all the sturdy vines they wanted. That greatly expanded the range of things they could build.

There were a lot of animals too. They had only spotted the horse-dragon that one time, but there were packs of pebies, which were these rabbit-like dog creatures, and they often saw ganaroes, which were like wild cows. Closer to the Tenryu Mountains were monkeys with fox-like faces. Judging from the distant howls, the scratch marks left on trees, and the droppings they occasionally came across, there were wolves and bears around as well. If such fierce predators were able to breed here, that meant the area had to have an abundance of prey.

They were at least ten, probably fifteen kilometers from Riverside Iron Fortress and the kobolds occupying it. Was that close enough to feel they were a threat or far enough away to be safe? Like in the valley in the foothills, they would have to remain as cautious as they had of the dragons that made the Tenryu Mountains their home.

On the third day at their camp in the shadow of the rocks, they tried walking five or six kilometers west to the Jet River. When they happened to look upstream, there was a massive creature swimming with its head above the water. It looked like a dragon. The whole group panicked and got out of there in a hurry. That was a whole thing.

On the fourth day, they found some interesting tracks about a kilometer east of their camp. There were multiple sets of footprints, along with marks like something had sat on the ground. They seemed to come not from a four-legged beast but some bipedal creature.

That night, Haruhiro, Setora, and Kiichi were standing guard next to a stove that had been built to conceal the light of its fire as much as possible. Suddenly, Kiichi turned toward the southeast, and his ears stood straight up.

Setora tried to say something. Haruhiro raised a hand to stop her, but she closed her mouth before she could speak.

There was a noise. Haruhiro heard it, too, but he didn't know what kind of noise it was. It wasn't an animal. He could sort of tell that. He had no proof. It was all a hunch.

Haruhiro waved to Setora and Kiichi, giving them a signal that meant *"Stay here. I'll go look."*

Setora nodded. Kiichi would likely obey her. Haruhiro moved away from the stove without a sound.

He didn't mind this sensation. It was like he was swimming through the darkness. You might even say he found it comfortable. The air at night suited Haruhiro better than the daytime. He even imagined he could touch things through the night air, feel their heat.

He searched all over but found nothing. He had to conclude there was no large animal nearby. However, even if there wasn't one now, there might have been at one point. For instance, something might have approached to scope out the group, but accidentally—or for reasons beyond its control—ended up making noise. It might have thought *Oh, no,* and run away.

There were footprints too. Whatever was going on, the group was going to have to be more cautious. Depending on the situation, they might have to abandon their camp in the shadow of the rocks. It would hurt, but if they had to do it, they shouldn't hesitate.

When they were talking about it over breakfast, they heard more than just a noise. They heard a man's voice.

"Volunteer soldiers?" the voice said.

"Huh?" Kuzaku picked up the large katana lying at his feet. "Wh-who's there?!"

"Do you think we'd answer honestly?" Setora took up her bow and looked to Haruhiro.

Haruhiro took a deep breath. Volunteer soldiers? The voice had asked if they were volunteer soldiers. Merry kept quiet and looked in the direction the voice had come from. It was to the southeast.

What were they to think of this? Or should they move rather than think?

We were careless. There were signs. We should have anticipated this could happen, Haruhiro thought for a moment, but was that really true? Hindsight was always twenty-twenty. Haruhiro wasn't an omniscient god or a genius. He was nothing but a plain, mediocre human, so even if he could have predicted this might happen, he couldn't have known all the concrete details. It wouldn't do him any good to lament not having been able to do something he never stood a chance of being able to do in the first place.

"If you're volunteer soldiers, please answer," the voice said.

"What do we do?" Kuzaku crouched as he asked Haruhiro.

Before Haruhiro could answer, the voice pressed for a response. "Your suspicion is inevitable, but we are not suspicious. If you are volunteer soldiers, we can work together."

Setora's brow furrowed. "'We'?"

"He's not alone," Shihoru whispered.

Merry looked at Haruhiro. "They could be remnants of the Frontier Army."

"I'll come over to you," Haruhiro told the owner of the voice. Then he quickly looked at each of his comrades. "Everyone, stay here. Just be careful."

Kuzaku gave him a "'Kay," but Setora gave him a look that seemed more exasperated than dissatisfied, and Shihoru seemed worried too.

"Hold on," Merry grabbed Haruhiro's arm. "Take me with you."

"No, but—"

"You have no memories, remember? Can you make a split-second decision?"

"She has a point." Setora nodded. "You two go together. Self-sacrifice is fine and all, but taken too far, it becomes insufferable and does more harm than good."

Haruhiro almost apologized despite himself, but managed to stop at just saying, "Right."

Merry headed toward the voice with him.

A single man appeared from the trees about thirty meters ahead of them. "Here," he said.

Haruhiro and Merry looked at one another. What kind of man was he? As far as Haruhiro was concerned, the man didn't look like he was dressed all that differently from them. He was considerably older, though. The guy had to be over thirty. He was bearded and wore a leather outfit, along with boots and a deep green cloak.

"I don't know him," Merry said dubiously. "I don't think the Frontier Army had soldiers like that. But he doesn't look like a volunteer soldier either..."

The man approached. "I'm with the Expeditionary Force from the Kingdom of Arabakia."

"Expeditionary Force?" Haruhiro furrowed his brow. "Merry, have you heard of them?"

Merry shook her head.

"But if he's not with the Frontier Army..." Haruhiro stepped forward, keeping Merry safely behind him.

The man came to a stop about ten meters away from them. The man didn't feel *clean*. His skin was dark with grime. Haruhiro was used to living in the great outdoors too, though, so he wasn't one to talk.

The whites of the man's eyes were yellowed and bloodshot, and his ungloved hands were awfully dirty. His nails were cut short. Also, when the man walked, he made almost no sound.

"We came from the mainland," the man said, then grinned. "If you're volunteer soldiers, that makes us reinforcements. I was expecting you would welcome us."

"Welcome..." Haruhiro mumbled, then responded with a smile. To be honest, he was trying to hide his confusion. He wanted to be able to process the information he had. That would take time.

"Why are you here?" Merry asked the man. "In a place like this?"

The man shrugged. He apparently either didn't want to answer, or couldn't. He looked pretty tough. Could they trust him? Haruhiro couldn't decide.

"I'm a scout. Basically, I'm at the bottom of the heap." He smiled with an implied *You know how that is, right?* "I have no authority. If you people accept, I'm to lead you back to camp. The commander, or someone working for him, will reveal any information you should be told."

Camp. Commander. Information. Haruhiro mulled over what the man said as he listened. "You were the one monitoring us last night, huh?"

"So you did notice." The man licked his bottom lip. "You're the same as me. A scout... No, they'd call you a thief out on the frontier, huh?" The man spoke politely enough, but there was a roughness in his gestures and expression. Even now, this man was evaluating Haruhiro and Merry. Here's what he had to be thinking: *If I have to kill these two, how am I going to do it?*

Haruhiro was thinking much the same thing, as a matter of fact. The man looked capable. But he didn't feel like an opponent they couldn't beat. With Merry here, it was two against one, but that wasn't why. The man was clearly underestimating Haruhiro. That meant there was an opening he could work with.

That said, perhaps the man had a good reason to be so relaxed.

"And if we—" Haruhiro started.

"And if you," the man took over for him, "are the sort of unscrupulous people who wouldn't welcome us, I'm afraid to say I'll have no choice but to eliminate you. If you're not a fool, I think you'll understand this is not an idle threat, and I say it because I can deliver on it."

"What do you mean...?" Merry whispered.

Basically, it meant the man, or rather the Expeditionary Force, or whatever they were, were a level or two above Haruhiro's group.

Haruhiro glanced past the man. He hadn't noticed before now, but that was because his attention had been on the person before him. The man had made sure it was. There were armed men here and there throughout the forest. They weren't standing in the open, and more than a few were sticking out halfway from behind trees or bushes.

Even at a glance, Haruhiro counted ten-ish. He put his hands up. "Of course we welcome you."

There were five in his group, plus Kiichi. These guys were calling themselves a military force, so there were presumably more than ten or twenty of them. They were working on a different scale.

"I mean, we welcomed you to begin with. Did it not look that way?"

"Oh, I could see it." The man gave him a mocking smile. "I came all alone last night, though. I was confident that if we came back in force, you would definitely welcome us. If you're going to have a party, the more the merrier, right?"

Haruhiro was the type that preferred a calm evening to a raucous celebration, but he didn't need to rock the boat now. "You're right."

"The name's Neal." The man walked over with large strides and extended his right hand. "You?"

Haruhiro took the man's hand. "I'm Haruhiro."

Neal pulled Haruhiro in close and whispered in his ear. "That's a fine woman you've got with you."

The blood rushed to Haruhiro's head.

Neal seemed to see right through him as he clapped Haruhiro on the shoulder with a smile. "That was a compliment."

Haruhiro and Merry returned to the camp with Neal. They explained the situation to Kuzaku, Setora, and Shihoru, and decided to pack up and head to the Expeditionary Force's camp.

The Expeditionary Force's camp was more than five kilometers from the rocks, in the forest to the southwest. It was pretty close to the Tenryu Mountains, but according to Neal, they had yet to be attacked by any dragons.

There were a good fifty tents pitched in the area, and armed soldiers lay about maintaining their equipment or resting. The groups of soldiers sitting in circles didn't look like they were just chatting. They were rolling wooden dice or doing something with a large number of short, wooden sticks. Gambling, maybe?

When the soldiers noticed Haruhiro and the others, they stared, whispered to their fellows, and let out mean-spirited laughs. Many of them were young, just a little older or even a little younger than Haruhiro and his group. There were a good number of middle-aged, maybe even elderly soldiers whose beards had gone half white too.

Frankly, they gave off a bad vibe. Haruhiro didn't know for sure, but there were probably regulations a military force needed to follow. These guys seemed slovenly. Haruhiro had been living in the wild, so he wasn't one to talk, but they looked like a bunch of barbarians.

Even under the indiscreet stares of all those soldiers, Setora seemed unperturbed. But Merry and Shihoru both looked disgusted.

"They've come a long way from their hometowns to serve the military, and... Well, everyone's on edge," Neal explained, smirking. "It may be a little bit too stimulating for the young ladies here, but put up with them, will you? It's not malicious."

"Stimulating, huh?" Kuzaku seemed pretty mad. "You sure it's not malicious? I'm having a hard time believing that."

Neal cleared his throat, then let out a low laugh, but he didn't respond.

They walked through the camp, which wasn't really divided up into sections, until they came to an area where some large tents were concentrated. There was a table and chairs around it; some people were sitting and others stood. These guys didn't seem like the rank-and-file soldiers.

Neal walked forward, dropped to one knee, and bowed his head. "General. I've brought them."

"Well done."

The man he called General was not unkempt like Neal and the other soldiers; he had grown a proper beard that he kept well-groomed. In terms of age, he looked forty or thereabouts, with red hair and sharp eyes. His armor was polished, and he wore a black fur cloak over the top of it. Plus, this red-haired general was tall, although not as tall as Kuzaku.

"You're surviving volunteer soldiers, huh?" He had a throaty, intimidating voice.

For a moment, Haruhiro hesitated. Should he kiss up to the man? Or just act normal? "Um, yes."

"What do you mean, 'Um'?"

"Yes." Haruhiro corrected himself. He broke into a cold sweat and grimaced a little. The guy was pretty scary.

The general looked over to another man, who was a short distance away, standing instead of sitting in a chair. "Do you know them, Anthony?" the general asked.

The man called Anthony shook his head. "No, General. I have no personal acquaintances among the volunteer soldiers. I know a number of them by name, though."

The general looked at Haruhiro with rust-colored eyes. "What is your name?"

"It's Haruhiro." It was probably best not to defy this man. He seemed kinda scary. Though he didn't want to be too subservient either. Where was this mentality coming from? Haruhiro didn't even know that himself. "The others are Kuzaku, Shihoru, Merry, and Setora. Also, the nyaa's name is Kiichi."

"I don't know them," Anthony said with a shrug. "I don't think they're like Soma, Akira, or Renji, who even the regular forces respected."

"Soma... Renji..." Merry whispered.

Both those names had come up in the stories Merry had told them.

"Renji enlisted at the same time as us," Haruhiro said, then paused a moment. "We're...members of Soma's guild, the Day

Breakers." He wasn't lying, as far as he knew. He just didn't re-member the details surrounding that either.

"Day Breakers?" The general looked to Anthony.

Anthony nodded. "The clan is something like a platoon in the military. Soma gathered capable volunteer soldiers to form the Day Breakers. Some of them, like Akira, Rock, and Io, were famous even among us in the Frontier Army."

"You're in the Frontier Army?" Haruhiro asked.

Anthony nodded. "That's right. Graham Rasentra, who was commanding the Frontier Army in Alterna, sent an envoy to the mainland to request aid. My men and I were the ones ordered to guard that envoy."

"We don't know the frontier," the general said, looking to those around him. "Anthony is a valuable guide. That is why, even though it meant departing as soon as he arrived, we had him ac-company the Expeditionary Force."

"I was born on the frontier, after all," Anthony said with a servile expression on his face. "I have no intention of living in peace and safety on the mainland. I meant to come back either way."

Haruhiro really couldn't have cared less about their situation, but he sort of got the picture. The Kingdom of Arabakia had once prospered north of the Tenryu Mountains, in the land they now called the frontier. However, when they were defeated by the Alliance of Kings led by the No-Life King, they fled south of the Tenryus. What they now called the mainland would have been called the frontier a long time ago.

The Kingdom of Arabakia's largest base in the frontier, Alterna, had suddenly been attacked. General Graham Whatshisface of the Frontier Army figured he couldn't defend it and had asked the mainland for reinforcements. In the end, the reinforcements came. Or they barely made it, rather.

"It looks like there's nothing but goblins in Alterna." Haruhiro lowered his eyes. It was best to convey this dispassionately. "There were orcs at Deadhead Watching Keep, kobolds at Riverside Iron Fortress, and there was no one at the Lonesome Field Outpost."

"We have that information," the general said, waving his hand.

Haruhiro didn't immediately understand what it was they wanted from him.

Anthony decided to help him out. "The general wants to speak with you personally."

Obviously, there was no way that they had anything personal to talk about. Anthony was telling him in a roundabout way that the general wanted to talk in secret.

Haruhiro glanced at his comrades, then approached the general. The general turned away from Haruhiro and started walking. That probably meant *Follow me.*

"The Kingdom of Arabakia no longer has any foothold in this frontier," the general said in a low voice as he walked along at a relaxed pace. "If the king and his favored retainers back on the mainland decide that the situation is too difficult to reverse, it will put you people in a somewhat difficult spot... And us too."

Haruhiro couldn't understand what the general meant if he was going to beat around the bush like this. He had no memories.

Was it better to keep that a secret? Or to be forthright and reveal it? He hadn't been able to consult his comrades about that yet. They'd have to make up their minds soon, but right now, it was probably not a good idea to bring it up.

Actually, he couldn't decide if it was a good idea or not. The situation was too complicated and delicate. He'd have to keep quiet for now. "Um, so, basically..."

"The king and his close retainers will almost certainly attempt to sever the mainland from the frontier permanently."

"Sever?"

"To make it impossible to travel from one to the other."

"I got that much." What was it? He felt like he'd heard something about this from Merry... *Oh, right.*

In the Tenryu Mountains, or maybe it was under them, there was this secret passage, the Something-or-Other Road. The people of the Kingdom of Arabakia had originally used that road to evacuate south of the Tenryu Mountains. However, they had also used it to send an army into the frontier and build Alterna.

Even now, people and trade flowed between Alterna and the mainland using that Something-or-Other Road. Or they had, until just recently. Whatever the case, if they knew where the Something-or-Other Road was, it would be possible to go from the frontier to the mainland and vice versa. The Expeditionary Force must have traveled through the Something-or-Other Road too.

The general stopped walking, so Haruhiro stopped as well. There were no tents around them, and no soldiers either. "If we cannot secure a base on the scale of Alterna, the king will surely destroy the Earth Dragon's Aorta Road."

Ohhh. That was the official name of the Something-or-Other road. "Destroy it?" Haruhiro said.

The general turned, leaning in a bit to bring his face close to Haruhiro's. "We're a ragtag band, as you can see. We need all the help we can get. You'll be cooperating, volunteer soldier. Don't say no. We have to worry about this information leaking out. If you won't obey, I'll have no choice but to kill you."

Grimgar
of
Fantasy and Ash

9 | Paradise Lost

THINGS HAD GOTTEN BAD. Well, they had been pretty bad from the moment they'd woken up without their memories, so panicking about it now wasn't going to help. Still, when you had a long streak of absolutely nothing going right, there was no getting around the fact that it was exhausting.

Haruhiro and his group had taken up their own unique positions in the Expeditionary Force's camp. They were given a tent in the same area as the red-haired general Jin Mogis and his associates, as well as Anthony Justeen, who was treated like a visiting staff officer. They needed clearance to leave that area.

When the Expeditionary Force moved, the group was, of course, obligated to move with them. Anthony had five subordinates who had come with him to defend the messenger. Formally, these men were the same as Haruhiro and his group. Basically, they were all members of the regiment that reported directly to staff officer and regimental commander Anthony.

They were under constant surveillance, but if they stuck their heads close together, it wasn't impossible for them to talk in secret.

Haruhiro waited until night to talk with the group. "So, about the memories thing. What do you think?"

"I don't think we should say anything," said Merry.

"That makes sense," Setora agreed. "My opinion is the same as Merry's."

"What do you think they're going to make us do?" Kuzaku asked. "The Expeditionary Force is here to take back Alterna, right?"

"So we're supposed to...help them?" Shihoru suggested.

Setora gave an unconvinced hum. "They want us to sneak into Alterna, don't they? I wasn't from here to begin with, but originally you people would have been well-suited for the job."

"Nah, but the place is full of goblins, right? No way we're getting in there..." noted Kuzaku.

"If I went on my own, I might be able to manage it." Haruhiro mused.

"But you don't remember it, right, Haru? Even if you could sneak in—"

"There wouldn't be much point, huh?"

"Even if that's not it, I'm sure they have uses for us. They can use us as disposable pawns."

"Setora-saaan..." Kuzaku whined.

"What?"

"Could you watch your phrasing a little more...?"

"I have no intent to change the way I speak or act. You people will have to get used to it."

"Nah, I'm fine with it, you know? I mean, I can take a verbal beating."

"Then what is the problem?"

"I'm not the only one here."

"I'm fine with it, too," Merry interjected. "The way Setora never holds back actually feels good."

"I think it's better than trying to sugarcoat things," Shihoru said.

"Yeah, I agree." Haruhiro said.

"Huh? So, what? There's no problem, then?"

"You were making a scene about nothing. Now reflect on what you've done and silence yourself for a while."

"Right, sorry..."

Even though he was bigger than any of them, Kuzaku was like everyone's little brother. Maybe he had the disposition of the youngest child in a family, though it was unclear if he actually had siblings.

Being watched felt obnoxious, but the Expeditionary Force had ample supplies, so thankfully the group was provided with enough rations and water for each of them. There was a logistics corps as well as personnel capable of repairing weapons and clothing. Mogis said they were a ragtag band, but in this respect, they were an organized military force.

When dawn broke, the Expeditionary Force began preparing to move.

According to their superior, Anthony, the Expeditionary Force was currently forty kilometers west of Alterna. They would approach over the next three days, then launch an operation to retake the town.

"Forty kilometers in three days..."

"We're moving with an army, remember," Anthony explained. "And we'll be crossing mountains along the way."

"Mountains? You mean the Tenryus?" Haruhiro asked.

"It's a range of mountains that juts north from the Tenryu Mountain Range. There's a risk of being eaten by dragons, but that's inevitable. If we were to take a route around the mountains, we'd be passing through the Quickwind Plains. With a force of this scale, it's highly likely we would be discovered by the enemy."

To be honest, Haruhiro had nothing but bad feelings about all this. The Expeditionary Force was technically an army, but even an amateur like him could see they had been hastily scraped together.

First, there was the low morale of the troops. General Mogis had given the order to prepare to move, so you would have expected them to pack up their tents right away, but some of the men were still sleeping, and others were taking their time eating and drinking. There was even one soldier who got beaten by a superior officer for stripping out of his equipment and being half-naked, and another who fell while climbing a tree and got injured.

The soldiers of the Expeditionary Force were so undisciplined that it left Haruhiro feeling a little shocked. These guys weren't even in the minority. The lion's share of the force was like this, and even the officers, who swaggered around like they were important, weren't much better. Because of that, as long as they didn't do anything especially egregious—like running around naked and shrieking—they wouldn't be scolded.

General Mogis must have given up on them, because he didn't say anything until quite some time after he gave the order. He did get impatient, though. He strode right up to one soldier and suddenly kicked him in the butt. "We're moving out. Get ready."

Now, as for whether that got the soldiers moving immediately, it did not. There were a few who started dismantling their tents without much enthusiasm, but more than half were just sitting there glumly, kicking the trees, or plucking the grass.

"Whoa..." Kuzaku started to smile, but he couldn't bring himself to. "You think this is okay?"

It clearly wasn't. When Haruhiro first saw the group, his impression had been that there were a lot of young men. Still, they all wore armor, and had swords or spears. He had figured that, while they might not necessarily be experienced, they were all presumably professional soldiers.

That might not have been true. He wanted to be wrong about this, but most of them might actually have been less capable than Haruhiro's own group. Based on their builds and the way they moved, most of these soldiers looked like nothing more than amateurs. Haruhiro couldn't possibly imagine them bravely facing the enemy, weapons in hand, fighting an intense life-and-death battle.

Noon had passed by the time the Expeditionary Force was more or less organized enough to leave. When that happened, the soldiers started to complain that they were hungry and demanded something to eat. General Mogis was a patient man. Without snapping, he decided that they would set out after lunch. But, ultimately, by the time the sun went down, the Expeditionary Force had dragged itself a mere five kilometers.

On the second day, they began moving early in the morning and still barely made it twelve kilometers. It looked like they would probably cross the mountains the next day—no, the day after that.

That night, Anthony gathered Haruhiro and the rest of his group. "You've got to be exasperated, huh?"

"Well..." Haruhiro avoided saying anything.

"I didn't know anything about the situation in the mainland either. I'm frontier-born, after all." Was Anthony being self-deprecating or looking down on the people who were mainland-born? His smile could have been read either way. "They'd told us how great the mainland was, though. Said it was a paradise, nothing like the savage frontier."

"You went there, right, Anthony...-san?" asked Kuzaku.

Anthony lowered his eyes and nodded with a frown. "When we came out of the Earth Dragon's Aorta Road, we entered a fortress called Spezia...and were detained there."

They had discriminated against him as a man of the frontier. That was what Anthony thought at first, but that apparently wasn't it. The number of mainlanders who interacted with Anthony and his men from the frontier had been kept to a minimum, and they'd said nothing about the mainland, not even responding to questions.

"When I joined the Expeditionary Force on the way back through the Earth Dragon's Aorta Road, General Mogis told me the truth," Anthony said with a sigh. "We were detained at Spezia because they didn't want people in the frontier to know about the situation in the mainland, because it was no paradise..."

It had apparently been around a hundred and thirty years, give or take, since the humans of the Kingdom of Arabakia escaped south of the Tenryu Mountains. Since then, the kingdom had colonized the south and gradually expanded their territory. They had made their return to the frontier roughly one hundred years ago and built Alterna.

Arabakians, like Anthony, who were born in the frontier—which was to say, in Alterna—were told this: There were not tens, but hundreds of cities with large populations in the southern lands. The fields stretched as far as the eye could see, and more livestock than could ever be counted grazed on the hills and at the base of the mountains. Because there were plentiful mines that produced iron, gold, and silver, the kingdom maintained an army that numbered in the tens of thousands, and even the commoners wore fabulous jewelry.

Even further south of the southern lands were barbarian tribes that had not submitted to the kingdom. But these primitives were nothing but savages. The mainlanders called them monkeys and called the war to subjugate them a hunt. It was rare for a soldier to die when out hunting. The barbarians fought among themselves, and the kingdom even stepped in to mediate between them sometimes. The king was a merciful father.

The mainland had developed industry, and the people lived in prosperity, so music, theater, and other forms of leisure were plentiful. The God of Light, Lumiaris, was widely worshiped, and the blessings of the light filled the land.

The currency used in Alterna was minted on the mainland. However, its value was completely different in each place. An object that cost one gold coin on the frontier could be bought for ten silver coins on the mainland.

In a way, there was no poverty on the mainland. Even if you lost all your wealth gambling, there were institutions that provided aid to the poor in the cities, and if you went to one of them, they would guarantee you food, water, and a roof over your head.

"It was all a big fat lie," Anthony said, gesturing to the soldiers of the Expeditionary Force who were lying around in the darkness, or drinking and partying. "What would these lowlifes be doing in paradise?"

According to General Mogis, the Expeditionary Force was made up of the second and third sons of farmers, street thugs, and deserters who had been captured.

Furthermore, there was only one town in the mainland that was fit to be called a city: the capital. The king, the royal family, his closest retainers, and a thousand other nobles, along with somewhere between one and ten thousand people to support these privileged classes, lived in New Rhodekia, the capital of the Kingdom of Arabakia.

There were countless farming villages, but they were taxed heavily, and the people's lives were difficult.

The war with the "monkeys" in the south was incredibly intense. Those savages were the reason they hadn't been able to build larger towns. The mainlanders were under constant barbarian attack and lived in fear of pillaging.

The Kingdom of Arabakia had warred with the savages for over a century, and not only had they failed to exterminate them, they hadn't even set foot in their strongholds to the south. The barbarians were divided into many tribes, so the kingdom would work with one tribe, having them fight another. Shrewd negotiation was how they had barely managed to maintain a hold on their territory.

In the farming villages, the eldest child inherited the farm, so the second and younger sons either eked out a living as tenant farmers or had to leave their village. The youths of the farming villages flowed into New Rhodekia with no way to feed themselves. However, only a select few could find any kind of work. Ultimately, about the only options they had available were to join a band of criminals or volunteer for the military.

The ferocity of the battlefields in the south led to constant desertions. There were dogs tasked with chasing down fleeing deserters. There was also the Black Hounds, a special operations unit specializing in the capture, reeducation, return, or even execution of deserters.

"After ten years killing savages all over the south, General Mogis was made commander of the Black Hounds," Anthony said with a sideward glance at the general's tent. "I don't know what he did to end up leading the Expeditionary Force. But judging by the quality of the troops he's been given, you can't say this was a step up the ladder."

According to Anthony, the Expeditionary Force was made up of a thousand men, including the logistics corps that supported them from the rear. However, with the exception of a few dozen men like Neal the scout, who had been one of General Mogis's proteges since his time in the Black Hounds, there were no decent soldiers in the lot. Even those with army experience were deserters from the south. They had captured a bunch of cowards who fled for their lives and shipped them off to the frontier.

Setora sighed. "This is going to be a real headache."

"Based on his military record, I think the general is capable," Anthony said in a low voice. "He must have something in mind."

It seemed there were a variety of people with their own intentions and situations, and Haruhiro and his group were caught up in the middle of it. He would rather not have gotten involved, but it was too late for that. The general had delivered a clear threat: If they didn't cooperate, they'd be killed.

The unmotivated soldiers were large in number but not particularly scary. However, the general's dozens of loyal subordinates were probably all experienced men like Neal. For now, they'd have to do as he said.

"Did he mention the bit about how they're going to destroy

the Earth Dragon's Aorta Road if the Expeditionary Force can't take Alterna?" Haruhiro asked.

Anthony nodded. "The general did say that. He probably revealed it to us because we're not mainlanders. It seems there are agents of the king hiding among the troops."

Those agents were under secret orders to observe the Expeditionary Force's actions and return to the mainland to report to the king if the situation warranted it.

For the King of Arabakia and the nobility, it wasn't the south that was paradise, but the frontier. If possible, they wanted to return here in triumph. Even now, a hundred plus years since they were driven out by the Alliance of Kings, they hadn't abandoned that dream.

But a dream was no more than a dream. The kingdom had its hands full just dealing with the barbarians who were running rampant. Even when Alterna fell, all they could muster was an unruly mob like this Expeditionary Force.

"If the enemy were to discover and take the Earth Dragon's Aorta Road, our Kingdom of Arabakia would be finished," Anthony said in a cynical tone. "I'm sure they're getting ready to cave it in before that happens, as a last resort."

If the Expeditionary Force was soundly defeated, the king's men would secretly break off and return to the mainland. If the king made the decision after hearing their report, the kingdom's dream would end, but they would be spared an invasion by the Alliance of Kings.

Kuzaku looked around. "So you're saying there're spies...?"

"Even as someone born on the frontier, I was raised to have pride as a man of the Kingdom of Arabakia," Anthony said in a pained voice. "For now, I just want to take Alterna back. It's my hometown, after all. My comrades who died can't rest in peace like this."

Haruhiro didn't know much about the king, the nobility, or the people of the mainland, but he wasn't completely unable to empathize with Anthony.

Still, could they really retake Alterna?

The next day they advanced five kilometers east, and the Expeditionary Force prepared to cross the mountains. There wasn't anything specific that needed doing. They were just going to rest early now that there was a mountain range in front of them that looked like it might harbor dragons.

Did General Jin Mogis really plan on taking back Alterna?

The day after that, the Expeditionary Force started climbing the mountains. The men acted scared, or masked it by fooling around, or complained about the tough climb. The ones around General Mogis were quiet, so they must have been from the Black Hounds, or they were other proper soldiers who had not been deserters.

Just how many men in this force could fight properly? Haruhiro tried to count, but excluding Anthony, his five subordinates, and Haruhiro's own group, there were maybe fifty of them at best.

As Haruhiro was climbing in a gloomy mood, Neal the scout came over to him. "Ever encounter a dragon before?"

Haruhiro looked at Merry. According to her, they had been attacked by an incredibly frightening dragon that spat fire and fought a small dragon called a wyvern. As for Haruhiro, he had apparently even ridden a dragon in some place called the Emerald Archipelago. Naturally, he remembered none of this.

While he was wondering how to respond, Kuzaku answered for him. "Well, yeah, a few times."

"The dragons in the Tenryu Mountains?" Neal asked.

"Nah." Kuzaku shrugged. "But a dragon's a dragon, right?"

"Don't tell me you've killed one."

"Not killed one, but rode it."

"What?"

"But not me. Haruhiro." Kuzaku was boasting for some reason.

Neal stared at Haruhiro. "You?"

"He may not look like much, but our leader's awesome." Kuzaku sounded proud this time.

No, I'm not that awesome, and what do you mean I don't look like much? Besides, man, you don't even remember it happening.

There were so many things to poke fun at, Haruhiro didn't know what to do. But since they were covering up the fact that they had no memories, he kept his comedic jabs to himself.

"I thought you seemed awfully calm, but that explains it, huh?" Neal smiled wryly. "If a dragon shows up, it's all yours. I've only seen them from a distance. Deep down, I'm scared silly."

"You don't look it," Haruhiro pointed out.

"I'm just acting tough in front of the ladies," Neal said casually.

Suddenly, Setora came to a stop. She looked to the south and narrowed her eyes.

Neal's face twitched. "Whoa, what is it? Don't tell me..."

Setora grinned. "Just kidding."

10 | Life and Death

THE MOUNTAIN wasn't especially steep, and the weather was good. The journey would have been just like a group climb, if not for the dragons. When a thousand or so people march in columns, wild beasts tend not to approach them—except for the mightiest of all animals, the dragon, said to have no predators but those of its own kind.

It took until evening to reach the summit, thankfully with no dragon sightings during that time.

Looking to the east, they saw a large city. Not Alterna. Damuro. In the time when the Kingdom of Arabakia prospered north of the Tenryu Mountains, Damuro was the central city of their southernmost region. When Damuro fell, the victory of the Alliance of Kings and the defeat of humanity was set in stone.

After that, Damuro became a goblin den, divided into the New City in the west and the Old City in the east. The Old City had been neglected for over one hundred years, and it was still in ruins. According to Merry, it was inhabited by those goblins who were defeated in the factional struggles of the city, along with other outcasts. The New City that had been rebuilt by the goblins was, in a word, bizarre. It looked more like a massive anthill than a city, with high-rise buildings mixed into the middle of it.

The Expeditionary Force headed east down the mountain, taking breaks along the way. They didn't want to spend the night on the mountainside, so even if the sun went down as they went, they would just have to keep going and pray for no dragons.

The soldiers had started out either jumping at their own shadows or messing around, but now they moved forward in silence. Even if they started whining, "I'm tired, I can't take anymore," nobody was going to carry them on their back or pull them along by the hand. If they didn't walk on their own two feet, they would be left on the side of a dragon-infested mountain.

Once they were over the peaks, the Expeditionary Force started to act a little more like a proper military. Could that have been why General Jin Mogis chose the route? Although, if dragons had shown up, there would have been too much chaos for the troops to learn any discipline, so maybe Haruhiro was overthinking it.

That's right. No dragons appeared. The Expeditionary Force finally finished descending the mountain late at night, and most of the soldiers collapsed wherever they were and slept like rocks.

Haruhiro and his group were exhausted, too, but they didn't go to sleep immediately. This was the time to prepare bedding, no matter how minimal, and rest themselves properly. If they went to bed hungry, their sleep would be shallow, so they had to eat something as well, and if they didn't quench their thirst, they wouldn't get quality sleep either.

While Haruhiro and the others were preparing to go to sleep, General Mogis walked calmly between the soldiers. The vast majority of the men were out cold and didn't stir. It was kind of eerie, the way the general looked like he was walking through a field of the dead. No, not kind of; it *was* eerie.

The general hummed as he went. He was blatantly enjoying himself.

"You sure that guy's not nuts?" Kuzaku whispered.

The general had chosen to cross the mountain, betting on no dragons appearing, in order to train his men. Maybe that wasn't it. He would have been fine with dragons appearing. In fact, he had wanted them to. The dragons would have attacked, and the men would have run left and right, panicking, as they were killed one after another. Had Jin Mogis wanted to watch that scene unfold, smiling and humming as he watched...?

That was absurd. Haruhiro was pretty tired, so he was probably just indulging in silly fantasies.

When the sun rose, Haruhiro woke immediately, but it took quite a while before the soldiers of the Expeditionary Force followed suit.

They set out at close to noon, and by the time they had marched four kilometers to the southeast, the sun was already going down. Alterna was still about ten kilometers due east.

From this point on, it was mostly groves of trees, open plains, and marshland. If they marched with an army of a thousand men, they would be spotted from a long way away. If they wanted to launch a surprise attack on Alterna, they had to cut across the land with a forced march at night and take it in one hard push.

General Mogis ordered the army to stand by, then called for Neal the scout, Anthony, and Haruhiro's group. "I have an important mission for you people to carry out. I want you to make contact with our agents who should be hiding in enemy territory, and to gather information."

"Hiding?" Haruhiro asked. "By enemy territory, you mean Alterna, right? Does that mean there're people in Alterna?"

The general merely stared at Haruhiro, not saying anything.

"If they haven't been found," Anthony answered. "In the case that Alterna was occupied by the enemy, a small number of people were to remain inside the town, waiting for support."

"That assumes they followed the rules," Neal added.

"Confirming that is part of your mission," the general said nonchalantly.

But it seemed dangerous. No, it was unquestionably going to be really dangerous. Honestly, Haruhiro didn't like it. But if those were the general's orders, he couldn't refuse. He thought for a moment before opening his mouth. "Maybe we should keep our numbers to an absolute minimum?"

The general was silent. He was looking at Haruhiro.

"I'm well-suited to the task, but if I bring people who aren't along with me, they'll only get in the way."

"I'm a priest," said Merry. "If anyone gets injured, I'll be useful. I think I should go too." Merry was probably no specialist at undercover operations, but there was the matter of their memories. Ultimately, Haruhiro was going to need her to come along.

"I..." Kuzaku started to say, then groaned. "I'd love to go, but I might cause trouble for you..."

There was no reason that they desperately needed Setora and Kiichi to come with them either.

"Okay, so me, Merry...Anthony-san, and Neal-san." Haruhiro looked at the general. "How's that?"

When Haruhiro looked into General Mogis's rusty eyes, he was struck with unease for some reason. The man's expression was hard to read. Was he plotting something horrible? Haruhiro couldn't help but suspect it.

The general nodded. "Very well. Set out at once."

Just as they were heading out, Kuzaku complained. "We're getting left behind, huh? I wanted to go too."

"You yourself said that you might cause trouble."

"Well, yeah. I might cause trouble for you, but I still want to be there. I know that's contradictory. But that's valid, right?"

"It's not." Setora didn't mince words. "Kiichi and I might be one thing, but you and Shihoru could end up weighing them down. Haruhiro made the right decision."

"But Setora-san, I don't think that's why Haruhiro did it. It's less that we'd be a hindrance, and more that, deep down, he's worried about us. It's that fatherly urge to keep us out of danger, you know? Oh, I guess he's not our dad, huh? It's just normal concern, then."

"No, man," Haruhiro told him. "It's that you'd just be in the way. You're huge."

"Oh, come on... Huh? Are you serious? I mean, I know I'm way too big, but still!"

Shihoru tugged on Haruhiro's sleeve. "Take care."

Haruhiro felt a little embarrassed and looked away. "Yeah."

"You, too, Merry," Shihoru added.

"I will," Merry said, her lips twitching to give her a slight smile. "Thanks."

The group of four set off soon after that.

Farms and pastures dotted the land south of Alterna, as well as farmhouses here and there, though not enough to qualify as a village. Now that Alterna had been taken, the fields had been torn up, and they saw no sign of livestock. The farmers had fled or been killed. Obviously, the houses were all empty. They saw no evidence of lurking goblins either.

After the sun went down, the group set foot inside one of the farmhouses. It was a solid wooden house with a thatch roof, but it looked no different from any of the others. The inside had been torn apart. No doubt that was the doing of orcs or goblins.

"Where is it?" Haruhiro asked Anthony.

"Over here." Anthony led Haruhiro to the kitchen. It wasn't separated from the rest of the house in any way. There was just an oven and a counter for preparing food in one corner of the room.

Anthony helped Haruhiro to move the kitchen counter aside. A secret door was hidden on the wall behind where it had been.

The hidden door opened to a cramped little room that stank of dust and mold. Barrels, boxes, and old tools had been left inside, but those had to be decoys. Anthony and Haruhiro pulled the barrels and other stuff out of the room, then peeled the stone tiles off the floor. Eventually, they revealed an entrance that resembled a well.

"It's fifty years old, from what I've heard," Anthony said as he wiped the sweat from his brow. "There are supposed to be others, too, but this is the only one that I know of."

"Feels like something's going to come out of it." Neal gestured to the passage with his chin. "You go first."

The group's marching order on the way down was Anthony, Haruhiro, Merry, and Neal at the end. They hooked their hands and feet on metal fixtures on the walls, but they had to proceed straight down for a while. It really was just like a well, and only big enough for a single person to fit through at a time.

"The fixtures have started to come loose in some places. Be careful—whoa!" No sooner had Anthony said that than he cried out in surprise. "That was dangerous. One of the fittings fell out."

Despite that, they all managed to make their way down the vertical portion. After that, there was a tunnel less than a meter across—low enough that even Haruhiro, who was not particularly tall, had to duck his head. He was forced to crouch as he walked, so it was pretty rough. Anthony, at the front of the group, was carrying a small lantern. That was their only light.

"They go into hiding and wait for reinforcements they can't even be sure will come, huh?" Neal snorted. "That's a losing stance if I ever heard one. I wouldn't take it, myself. Let's hope the people of the frontier have a little more backbone."

"The people of the frontier," Anthony said with a stern tone, "have steadier nerves than you mainlanders. That much is certain."

Neal laughed a little. "You could be right."

"I am."

The tunnel had been devised to avoid places where the rock was too hard to dig through. It twisted and turned. There was no telling when it would end. Haruhiro occasionally checked on Merry. Each time, she nodded to him as if to say she was fine.

"Where does this connect to?" Haruhiro asked Anthony.

"The dread knights' guild in West Town."

"The dread knights... West Town..." Haruhiro repeated pensively.

As he recalled, Merry had told them that a former comrade of theirs, Ranta, had been a dread knight. West Town. He wasn't sure, but it was probably the western side of Alterna. Maybe that was obvious.

"Judging by how far we've walked, we should be under Alterna by now," said Anthony.

They walked a good distance farther after that. When they came to a rock wall, Anthony stopped.

Neal let out a bitter laugh. "Oh, come on..."

"Don't jump to conclusions." Anthony stopped crouching and stretched out his back. Wouldn't he hit his head? No, it looked like the ceiling was finally higher. Anthony hooked the lantern to his waist. "Okay, we'll have to climb. Follow me."

Unlike at the entrance, there were no metal fittings here, so they had to push their hands and feet against the walls and slowly work their way up.

After about two meters, the passage connected to a hole that went horizontally. If they crawled, they would just fit into it. The hole was even tighter than the tunnel they had just come through, but it was reinforced with stone.

"This is the exit," Anthony said, then began to bang on something. Was it blocked with only a thin barrier of stone? Anthony knocked it out with brute force.

When they came out, they were in a large, open room made from stone. Anthony took the lantern from his waist and held it in his hand, shining it around.

Were those statues lining the wall? Figures that were not quite human or beast stood on top of pedestals. They came in a variety of sizes. Some were the size of a person while others were half that.

Then there was a creepy thing that Haruhiro couldn't identify at first. He thought it was the dead body of some creature, but it was a candle. Countless candles had melted and then hardened together, assuming this frightful form that now dominated the floor of this room.

"Skullhell worship, huh?" Neal looked at one of the statues and shrugged. "It's distasteful. Humans, worshiping the god of death."

Anthony looked like he was about to say something.

Haruhiro tensed. He'd drawn his dagger without noticing it. "Is someone there?"

Way in the back of the room...was that a statue too?

No. That was no statue. It moved. Stood up. "O-O-O-O Darkness, O-O-O-O L-Lord of V-V-Vice."

It spoke. That was a human voice.

"A survivor?!" Neal drew his dagger and prepared himself.

"No..." Anthony lowered his lantern to the ground and pulled out his sword.

"It's not!" Merry shouted.

"D-D-Demon C-C-Call," someone said in an incredibly hoarse voice.

A purple, cloud-like thing began to form a vortex in the darkness. That whirling mass soon took on a specific form. It had a head like a pure-white deer and an emaciated human body covered in a dark cloak. What was that thing?

"A demon!" Merry said. "A dread knight's familiar!"

"What's going on?!" Neal shouted.

Merry didn't answer him. "Stop the demon! I'll purify it!"

Purify it... A zombie, huh?

The No-Life King's curse had transformed that dread knight into a moving corpse. It wasn't a survivor. It was already dead.

"Wahhehhhahhhhhhhhh!"

The demon let out a terrifying cry as it charged. The white, bone-like arms that had been hidden by its cloak came into view. Its hands were practically scythes.

"Hahh!" Anthony let out a battle cry as he knocked the demon back with his sword.

Haruhiro and Merry looked at one another. What was Merry trying to do, and what did she want from Haruhiro? He understood in an instant.

Haruhiro ran past Anthony, who was trading blows with the demon, and the dread knight zombie noticed him.

"Ah, ah, ah, ah."

The zombie had a weapon. A curved sword, a scimitar. Not just one, but two. A dual-wielder, huh? When the zombie stepped forward, Haruhiro got chills.

He'd assumed that because it was a zombie, it would be slow and stupid, or at least not as quick as it had been while alive. Maybe it had been faster before, but it was still pretty quick, despite being dead.

In the time it took Haruhiro to say "Whoa," it had closed the gap.

His body reacted instinctively. He blocked the two scimitars with his dagger and turned them aside, but he had no idea how he managed it. The zombie kept coming.

Oh, crap. Oh, crap. Oh, crap. Oh, crap. Oh, craaaap.

Haruhiro drew the other dagger, the one with a wavy blade that looked like flames. With it, he just barely deflected the zombie's scimitar. *Wow, I can actually do this, huh?* he thought in surprise.

However, the zombie suddenly vanished before his eyes.

"Huh…?" The left. He didn't know if it was instinct, or what, but Haruhiro looked to his left.

There it was. The zombie.

Did it teleport? No way, that's absurd. Uh-oh. The scimitar. I can't avoid it, and I can't deflect it either. I'm not gonna make it.

"O Light, may Lumiaris's divine protection be upon you." Merry came at the zombie like she was going to tackle it.

That was just what they'd been after. No, he hadn't signaled her, and he'd been in danger, but it had been their intent all along that Haruhiro would act as a decoy to catch the zombie's attention, then Merry would purify it with magic.

"Dispel!"

There was a burst of light that engulfed the zombie. When the zombie fell, the demon vanished too.

"Haru!" Merry rushed over to him, a terrible look on her face. "Are you hurt?!"

"Oh... Yeah." The way she grabbed his arm tight and touched his face surprised him a little. "I'm fine. Thanks."

Merry let out a sigh. "Thank goodness."

"So this is one of those zombies I've been hearing about?" Neal kicked the fallen zombie, trying to turn it over.

"Don't," Anthony stopped Neal. "He was being manipulated by a curse."

"Hah," Neal laughed derisively. "'He'? The curse, or whatever it was, is broken now. It's just a dead body."

"Do you mainlanders have no respect for the dead?"

"I don't know how it is in the frontier, but Skullhell worshipers deserve nothing but contempt, even once they're dead. These guys are vile, okay?"

"From what I can tell, he was a lord of the dread knights' guild. He stayed in Alterna and fought to the last. What's vile about that?"

Neal waved his hand to cut off the conversation, acting as if it was too much bother.

Merry knelt next to the body and offered a prayer. Anthony offered a silent prayer of his own too. Haruhiro tried to emulate them, but was there any point in keeping up appearances when he didn't really mourn the man?

"You're the same as me, huh?" Neal gave him a friendly slap on the back.

I don't know about that, thought Haruhiro, but he said nothing. He had a feeling he was never going to like Neal. Yeah, he might have really hated the guy.

"Let's go." Anthony picked up the lantern he had placed on the ground. "We have business at the thieves' guild. It's in West Town, too, so it's not far."

The dread knights' guild was under an abandoned house that looked like it could collapse at any moment. The above-ground portion looked run-down at a glance, but the structure was solid, the halls were intricate, and there were many small rooms. It had many hidden rooms, and one of them contained a passage leading to the underground.

That lord had likely been wounded in battle and fled into the dread knights' guild only to die there. However, even after occupying the city, the enemy had not found the guild. Their group searched above and below ground just to be sure, but there were no survivors, obviously, and no other zombies or even dead bodies to be found.

That lord had been the only one to die underground and then be turned into one of the moving dead by the No-Life King's curse. Thus he had been there, waiting, when their group arrived.

"Looks like we did a good deed, as followers of Lumiaris, the God of Light," Neal said brazenly. "That Skullhell-worshiping heretic had turned into an abomination in defiance of the natural order. It was a vile being that needed to be destroyed. I'm sure Lumiaris must be quite pleased."

"Would you please shut up?" Anthony glared at Neal. "I don't sense any now, but we can't be sure there are no enemies about."

Neal put on a faint smile and raised his hands in mock surrender.

The area was dimly lit. Sunrise was approaching. West Town was the slums, and the buildings looked old, dilapidated, broken, or on the verge of collapse, but they had somehow been preserved with maintenance.

The group still hadn't seen so much as a single goblin since coming up to the surface. Were there no goblins in West Town? No, they were probably just inside, sleeping. They had to get to where they were going before the goblins woke up.

"It should be around here." Anthony looked to Haruhiro. "Why haven't we gotten there yet?"

Don't ask me was how Haruhiro really felt, but he was a thief. He couldn't reveal that there was no way he could tell them where the thieves' guild was.

"Because...it's the thieves' guild?" Haruhiro tried suggesting.

"Because...it's morning?" Merry offered, but Haruhiro wasn't so sure that helped much.

He put on a frown that he hoped looked right. "It's kinda been a long time, you know...?"

Neal looked around. "It *is* an awfully suspicious place."

Their group had focused their attention on an odd building that was a complex mix of stone and wood, and they were trying to circle around it to find an entrance. The problem was, they couldn't. They ran into walls and fences—among other obstacles—and just couldn't seem to find any way to get around to the side or back of the building. They tried heading into the nearby alleyways but were still unable to get through to the other side, and they ended up having to turn back.

"Hold on..." said Haruhiro. *We're getting lost, aren't we?*

They were on a narrow road that ran next to the building in question, but Haruhiro didn't know where they were. If he wanted to get back to, say, the dread knights' guild from here, he would probably have had a surprisingly hard time. It wouldn't be easy, at least.

Anthony sighed. "This is bad."

Even now, time was going by. Haruhiro pulled on his earlobe. He felt no less of a sense of urgency than Anthony, but the more he tried to hurry, the more likely he was to miss things, and the more the urgency dulled his thinking. He needed to stay calm here.

That was when, suddenly, a voice spoke from behind him, leaving him flabbergasted.

"Do you people need something?" It was a woman's voice.

It came from behind them, which meant the woman was in the alley that the group had just been down. When had she arrived there? Where had she appeared from? Haruhiro hadn't noticed her at all. He turned around.

It was a woman, like he thought. She looked nothing if not human. Her long hair hid half her face.

Her body, on the other hand, was not hidden. She wasn't naked, but it would have been more appropriate if what she wore did a better job of covering her. She was showing too much skin.

"Oh..." Neal took a deep breath.

Anthony gulped.

Merry tried to say something, but the woman spoke first.

"Old Cat," she said. The woman's eyes went wide as she stared at Haruhiro. She seemed surprised.

I'm the one who's surprised here, okay? "Huh?" Haruhiro pointed at himself. "Ol...cat?"

The woman brushed her hair back behind her ear and sighed. "You're still alive?"

"Alive..." *Olcat? No, was it "Old Cat"?*

It wasn't clear what she was referring to, but she probably knew who Haruhiro was. Haruhiro, however, didn't know her. He didn't remember.

"Alive..." Haruhiro lowered his gaze. "Well..."

For now, it was best not to mention anything he shouldn't. But on the other hand, it wouldn't be good if she thought he was

hiding or trying not to talk about something. "I made it some-how, thanks..."

"I heard you'd gone missing. I was sure you were dead."

"Stuff happened."

"I am Anthony Justeen, a regimental commander in the 1st Brigade of the Arabakia Kingdom's Frontier Army," Anthony introduced himself. "You're with the thieves' guild, right? So you made it through all right..."

"All right, huh? *I don't know about that*," the woman whispered, crossing her arms. "The name's Barbara. I'm a thief, so that's just my work name."

Merry leaned in and whispered in Haruhiro's ear. "That person... She might be a teacher, though that's just a guess on my part. You used to call her 'Sensei.'"

"Sensei..." This made less and less sense.

Barbara was looking at Haruhiro again. If he got too flustered or looked away, she might get suspicious, but for some reason, he couldn't bring himself to look at her directly.

Why did this thief, Barbara, who was supposedly his teacher, not wear proper clothes? What was it that she'd been teaching him?

It was too much of a mystery.

11 | Hidden Meaning

T HE STRUCTURE OF THE DREAD KNIGHTS' guild had been pretty unique, but the thieves' guild was even weirder. The entrance Barbara led them to was an extremely low, rusted iron door. The design carved into the center of it—a palm with a keyhole—must have been the symbol of the guild. Without grasping, pushing, or pulling the handle, Barbara unlocked the door and opened it. How did that even work? Haruhiro had no idea.

When they passed through the door, they entered a narrow corridor with shelves on either side, and when they went around the corner, they were forced to turn their bodies sideways to continue. Past that was a dead end, but they were able to climb a rope to the other side of the ceiling. They crawled through the cobweb-filled attic and descended into another corridor before going up and down some stairs to finally reach a room with no floor. Well, no, it did have a floor, but it was way down below— far enough down that Haruhiro was hesitant to jump. On closer inspection, however, there was a ladder, and they used it to climb down instead.

"Have a seat wherever," Barbara said, indicating one of a number of couches in the dimly lit room, then sitting on a desk with her legs crossed. "Our thieves' guild has been remodeled a little since the fall of Alterna. It may seem a bit inconvenient, but you get used to it when you live here."

"How many are left?" Anthony approached Barbara instead of sitting down. "Has anyone outside the thieves' guild survived? What happened to the Frontier Army? What of General Graham Rasentra? Did the Margrave survive? And what about the volunteer soldiers...?"

"Ooh, really laying it on me, aren't you? Everything requires a little foreplay, you know?"

"F-foreplay?" Anthony backed away in confusion. "Sorry. I see. Foreplay... Well, there is an order to these things, and that's important, of course. I was simply too hasty..."

"Well, aren't you cute?" Barbara chuckled and re-crossed her legs the other way. "The Margrave is apparently alive, held captive in Tenboro Tower, but we haven't been able to confirm it. General Rasentra was killed in a one-on-one duel with an orc named Jumbo. The Frontier Army was wiped out. Alterna is infested with goblins. The situation sucks, and I'm frustrated as hell. Maybe you want to go a round with me later?"

"Th-that's..." Anthony glanced at Haruhiro and the others sitting on the couches, then shook his head. "I'm not entirely against it, but I feel like...I shouldn't..."

"People screw. It's natural, okay? What do you have to hold back for?"

"Well, yes, but... Wait, really?"

"Are you gonna do me or not? You're a man! Be clear!"

"F-fine, I'll do you."

"Hold up!" Neal said, standing up from his couch in an angry huff. "Forget that novice! Do it with me!"

"Who're you calling a novice?!" Anthony shouted.

"With you, huh?" Barbara took one look at Neal, then licked her lips. "You're not my type, but you know what, that actually turns me on more."

"When I'm done with you, your body will never want any other man again."

"I like your spirit. But men who talk too much tend to leave you disappointed. I'm speaking from experience, here. I hope you won't be one of them."

What were these people talking about? Well, he knew *what* they were talking about, but why had it come up? If Barbara was Haruhiro's teacher, just what kind of initiation had she put him through?

"Um..." Merry raised her hand.

Barbara, Anthony, and Neal all looked at Merry in unison. Merry accepted their stares with a slight smile on her face. "If you want to relieve your frustration, go right ahead. But do it later. We came all this way to get as much accurate information as we could to retake Alterna."

Anthony and Neal said nothing, just got a little awkward.

"Oh, that's good," Barbara grinned at Merry. "I really like that. I like girls like you. Actually, you might be the closest to my type here. Want to have some fun?"

Merry glared at Barbara. "No way."

"Mmm..." Barbara writhed with pleasure. "Now you've got me even more fired up."

Merry scowled and shook her head. "What is with you?"

Seriously, Haruhiro wanted to agree, but he wasn't sold on criticizing his teacher. He didn't know what their relationship had been like before he lost his memories, so maybe it was best if he kept quiet.

"Well, let's stop joking around for now." Barbara jumped down from the desk and beckoned to Haruhiro. "This way, Old Cat. There're some things I want to check before we deal with your business."

"Me?"

"That's right. It's our first meeting as master and student in a long time. You must have a thing or two to tell me about, right?"

"No, not really..." Haruhiro glanced sideways at Merry. He had nothing to tell Barbara about. He couldn't possibly have. *What should I do?*

Merry seemed confused, too, and tilted her head to the side a little. *Doesn't look like you can avoid it,* her expression said.

Haruhiro stood up. "Okay...Barbara-sensei."

"Good. Over here. You know where I mean." Barbara walked over to the wall.

Suddenly, she vanished. That was how it looked.

"Huh?" Haruhiro chased after Barbara. He touched the wall, and it wasn't a wall at all. It looked like a wooden wall at a glance, but it wasn't. It was soft. Cloth? It was just designed to look like a wall.

He walked through the curtain designed to look like a wall and entered a little room behind it adorned with wall-mounted lamps...and nothing else. No Barbara either.

"Damn, what is this?" There had to be some trick to it. He tried all sorts of things and found that one of the walls turned. It was pitch dark on the other side. "Is this...?"

"Old Cat," Barbara's voice came from beside him. She was right next to him.

"S-Sensei?"

"Are you really Old Cat?"

"What do you mean?"

"You don't know me, do you?"

"Th-that's absurd."

"When I first met you, I never expected you to live long."

Barbara felt so close he could touch her, but at the same time far away. Was she moving? He wasn't sure. He couldn't tell.

"Gradually, I started to think you might actually have promise. When I heard you might have bit it down in the Wonder Hole, I was uncharacteristically disappointed."

"Sorry."

"That was four years ago now."

"Four years..."

"I heard a rumor that the Typhoon Rocks ran into you after that, but nothing since. I had to assume you'd died after all, you know?"

"Yeah...that's fair."

"Do you not remember, maybe?"

"Huh?"

"Tell me honestly."

Something wrapped around his throat. A hand. It felt cold. Probably Barbara's.

"What happened? No... Something happened, and you don't remember me. That, or it's a different person inside you."

Did she know something? She might have some idea. If not, she wouldn't think he'd forgotten, or that he had no memory of her. "Th-the Forbidden Tower," Haruhiro said, and the hand around his neck tightened. Haruhiro grunted and had trouble breathing, but Barbara quickly loosened her fingers.

"Continue."

"I woke up there. Underground. In the Forbidden Tower. When I did, I didn't remember anything but my name. Merry and the others—my comrades—and Io were there too."

"Io. Of the Day Breakers?"

"I don't remember anything about that. There was also Hiyomu—"

"Ohh...the woman who likes to act younger than she is, huh?"

"Hiyomu was there too. She was acting like she had no memories either. But it was a lie. It was like...she was trying to trick us."

"Trying to trick you?"

"Well, not her, but her master? I guess? There was someone she called 'Master.' That guy was apparently the one who stole our memories. She said if we wanted her to explain everything, we had better do what she told us."

"Stealing memories? That's possible? Was it a relic? But still..."

"Oh, but Merry, who came with us, didn't lose her memories. Because of that, everyone but Io, Gomi, and Tasukete turned down Hiyomu's...offer? It was more of a threat, though."

"Then, after a whole bunch of other stuff, you met me again, huh?"

"Yeah... But like you said, I don't remember you."

"Is that Anthony guy with the Frontier Army?"

"He said he escorted a messenger to the mainland."

"And Neal?"

"One of the reinforcements from the mainland... He's a scout with the Expeditionary Force, or something like that."

"So this Expeditionary Force is trying to retake Alterna?"

"It seems to be."

"Honestly, I wasn't holding out hope for it, but it looks like the mainland has made their move on schedule, Old Cat."

"Yes. Um..."

"What?"

"What is that 'Old Cat' stuff about?"

"Thieves call one another by work names. It's tradition. As your instructor, I gave you your name."

"Old Cat...?"

"Because you've got the eyes of an old cat."

"Ahh."

"When a cat's lived a long time, it never misses a trick. They're always aloof, living life as it suits them. It was my hope that you'd survive and become that sort of thief. I never told you that before, though."

Haruhiro didn't remember a thing, so it shouldn't have made him feel anything when she told him that, but for some reason, it did. He was scared that his emotions would lead him to make bad decisions, but this woman was his teacher. He owed her a debt of gratitude.

Barbara finally removed her hand from Haruhiro's throat and stroked his cheek. "Just how many of my thieving students are left now?"

"What, uh...happened to the volunteer soldiers?"

"About that..."

"Yes?"

"We need to think things through here. Can we trust the mainland? We also don't know if the Expeditionary Force's goals are the same as the mainland's."

Haruhiro's teacher was apparently a cautious, thoughtful person. How old was she? Haruhiro didn't really know, but he was certain she was a lot older than he was. She was probably experienced in a whole lot of ways, and she had plenty of information that Haruhiro and the others either didn't or couldn't possibly ever have had. He'd be lying if he said he wasn't hesitant, but he figured that she was someone he ought to trust. "Sensei?"

"Hm?"

"The general of the Expeditionary Force said that if they can't retake Alterna or Riverside Iron Fortress, the mainland is probably planning to seal the Earth Dragon's Aorta Road."

"The mainland and the Expeditionary Force aren't a monolith, then, huh?"

"I have no guarantee that the general was telling the truth, so I can't say with any certainty. But looking at the quality of the Expeditionary Force and their low morale, and factoring in Anthony's speculation following his visit to the mainland, I think it's true."

"The mainland doesn't want to lose the frontier. However, they don't intend to take risks and throw good resources after bad to recover it either."

"It looked like most of the soldiers in the Expeditionary Force were deserters or thugs."

"Getting rid of nuisances, huh? What was their commander like?"

"Is it best if I tell you everything now?"

"Of course. Tell me all of it, in as fine detail as you can. I want to talk business."

"That's fine, but...if I explain it all to you from the beginning, it will take a fair bit of time. Won't they think we're up to something weird?"

"Let them think that the student and teacher met up again after a long time and had a passionate fling."

"Uh, them thinking that we did that is kind of what I'm worried about."

"Ohh, Merry, was it? Is she your woman?"

"No. I'd never be a good match for her. Just look at me. It's obvious."

"Oh, you silly boy."

He suddenly felt something soft pressed against the area between his chin and lips, and heard a *smooch* sound.

"Wh-wha...?!" Haruhiro touched that spot. It was faintly moist. "Wh-what are you doing, Sensei?"

"There's nothing wrong with a handsome face, obviously. But a man is more than that."

"Maybe there's more wrong with me than my face? I've got no memories, after all."

"It's not for you to decide if you're good enough or not. That's up to your partner. I, for one, would like a taste of you myself."

"You're joking again...right?"

"You think so?"

Barbara's seriousness—and what happened between her and her student in that room—is something that will have to be left to the imagination. Whatever the truth of the matter, third parties will have to fly on the wings of speculation and come up with a scenario that seems likely to them.

After a not-so-short amount of time had passed, Haruhiro and Barbara returned to the room where the other three were waiting. The atmosphere in the room was something else.

"You took a while." That was all Anthony said, but as he sat there on top of the desk, he looked kind of sullen.

Neal, who was sitting on a couch with his legs spread and

elbows rested on his knees, clicked his tongue audibly. "You've got a look on your face like you just blew a load or three, huh? Just the two of you get to relieve yourselves? That's not funny. I can't stand this."

Merry was sitting on another couch, clasping her hands uneasily. When she saw Haruhiro's face, she immediately looked down.

"U-um...Haru."

"Wh-what?"

"I'm, uh..."

"Y-yeah?"

"We're not children anymore, so..."

"Well... Yeah, I guess? We're not children... Huh?"

"We're adults. I won't say anything. To anyone. Anything I shouldn't. So...it's okay."

She'd misunderstood. Even Merry had fallen victim to her imagination, and she was convinced something happened that never had.

"Whoa, huh?! You're wrong!"

"You *would* say that," Neal said with a smirk. "It's easy to say. Whether it's true or not."

Anthony hit the desk in frustration. "What thieves do together is none of my business. It doesn't matter."

Haruhiro slumped his shoulders. "It does matter..."

"I've more or less heard the situation." Barbara stroked Haruhiro's chin. "From my boy here. At length."

"Senseeii..."

"Whaaat?" Barbara said in an awfully syrupy voice. "You haven't had enough? You naughty boy."

She was having way too much fun. She was totally playing with him. Haruhiro looked at Merry, who was mumbling to herself and nodding again and again, like she was trying to convince herself of something. How was he going to clear up this misunderstanding?

"It's impossible, isn't it?" Haruhiro muttered. His head hurt.

12 | The Trick to the Lottery Is Not to Play

THE FALL of Deadhead Watching Keep had hit the Frontier Army in Alterna like a bolt from the blue, though there had been ominous whisperings between the volunteer soldiers before that. They said that orcs and undead from all over had been gathering in Rhodekia, the former capital of the Kingdom of Arabakia, now apparently called Grozdendahl; that a horde of orcs, or perhaps undead, may or may not have been sighted marching south from Grozdendahl; and that black smoke had risen from the Shadow Forest where the elves lived. There had been a major fire there, but not *just* a fire. The Shadow Forest might have been put to the torch.

The Frontier Army sent out scouts and tried to figure out the situation, but they were ultimately unsuccessful. They failed to detect the Alliance of Kings' offensive until Deadhead Watching Keep fell.

However, at that point, the commander of the Frontier Army—General Rasentra—was already in crisis mode. The moment he received a report of the keep's fall, he ordered a request for reinforcements to be sent to the mainland.

But it was too late. Two days after the fall of Deadhead Watching Keep, the enemy's reach extended to Alterna.

Despite Alterna's attempts to harden their defenses, their walls were easily broken. The enemy were far greater in number than they had imagined, and incredibly fierce. It wasn't just the Frontier Army; the volunteer soldiers who happened to be in Alterna at the time fought too. But they couldn't stop the enemy's momentum.

The enemy surrounded Tenboro, the home of Margrave Garlan Vedoy, in no time. Graham Rasentra tried to take a unit of his finest men into Tenboro, but he failed to accomplish his goal and died in single combat against an orc named Jumbo.

The enemy broke into Tenboro, and everyone but the Margrave himself was killed. It was said that brigadier generals Ian Ratty and Jord Horn died in battle as well.

There were three brigadier generals in the Frontier Army, men tasked with the authority to lead a brigade. The last of them, Wren Water, was unaccounted for, but it was presumed that he had fled Alterna for fear of his life or had been slain in the attempt.

The volunteer soldiers, under the command of Volunteer Soldier Corps Office Chief Britney, had fought a hard battle, and were said to have pushed the enemy back in places. The exploits of Renji, who had enlisted at the same time as Haruhiro, were renowned, and he had slain a great many enemies all by himself.

However, when a great horde of goblins rushed in from Damuro, the volunteer soldiers were washed away and exterminated.

It was all over in the span of a single night. After the battle ended, Barbara stayed in Alterna, as had been agreed upon. She gathered information while searching for survivors, but unfortunately she got no results.

According to Barbara, half the enemy force had left a few days after the fall of Alterna. Since then, the goblins had become masters of the city. The goblins' clean-up operation, the human hunt, was harsh and thorough.

There had actually been a number of people unable to escape who either holed up in buildings, or who had gone into hiding with heavy wounds, like the lord of the dread knight's guild.

That lord had been the exception. Most were found, dragged out, and massacred. The goblins lined up piles of human corpses in the plaza outside Tenboro and held something like a festival.

The bodies of the deceased weren't just put on display, though. Barbara had seen the goblins cutting the bodies into pieces, cooking, and boiling them. She had, of course, also seen the goblins eating them, albeit from a distance.

However, the goblins used all corpses the same way. Or, to be more specific, the only bodies they destroyed, taking out their rage and scorn on them, were the human ones, but they made meals of their own kind too. Therefore, this was a common, everyday occurrence for the goblins. It was their culture.

Barbara had to conclude that Alterna's human population had been wiped out. That seemed to be what the goblins thought too.

In the beginning, the goblins had been managed by an individual who stood about one hundred and fifty centimeters tall, a giant by their standards. Barbara called him the king, and the goblins weren't just respectful toward him; they groveled in his presence. When the king ordered something, they all either moved or stopped and fell silent. He dressed almost like a human, wore a crown made from some kind of reddish metal, and carried a staff of the same material.

Barbara had witnessed the goblins bowing before the king, repeatedly calling him Mogado. Mogado Gwagajin. That must have been his name or title.

There were also large goblins who carried equipment made of the same red metal who followed the king around and gave orders to the other goblins. They were clearly his entourage. Because there were about a hundred of them, Barbara called them the Hundred.

Once the human hunt and the nightmarish festivities that followed were over, the king appeared satisfied and left Alterna with about half of the Hundred.

There was another goblin who might have been his second-in-command. This one dressed like the king, but with no crown, and he took over after the king left. Barbara had heard the goblins call this individual Mod Bogg, or simply Mod.

Her guess was that "Mod" was a title, and Bogg was the individual's name. If this Bogg was next in rank to the king, you might call him something like a viceroy.

Alterna was ruled by Viceroy Bogg and twenty of the

Hundred, and thousands of goblins lived there under him. Specifically, Viceroy Bogg seemed to be living in Tenboro. The Hundred also stayed there, and they came out when they had business to attend to.

Barbara had seen the Margrave just once, bound with chains. He had been dragged around the plaza, mocked by the goblins, spat on, then taken back inside Tenboro. She couldn't say for sure that he was still alive, but if they were going to kill him, that would have been the time to do it. She surmised they might be keeping him captive for a reason.

No further goblins left Alterna, but the reverse was not true. The new arrivals were probably coming from Damuro. Their numbers were steadily increasing. These goblins were armed, and it seemed that nearly all of them were male.

Not many of the goblins appeared to be married. Of the goblins in Alterna, the viceroy and influential males like the members of the Hundred were, on very rare occasions, seen together with what must have been female goblins.

The female goblins had small heads, large breasts, and swollen bellies. They may have been pregnant. It was apparently standard in goblin society for an influential goblin to take multiple females as wives.

Whatever the case, the viceroy and the members of the Hundred who ruled Alterna in place of King Mogado Gwagajin lived in Tenboro Tower along with their wives. If there was a crisis, a messenger would run to Tenboro, and the Hundred would generally head out to handle it.

Tenboro had fallen. The door that had been destroyed at the time was removed and a barricade erected in its place. There were always dozens of goblins on the barricade, sometimes including members of the Hundred.

"If we go about it right, it sounds like we could take it," General Jin Mogis muttered, a dull glimmer in his rusty eyes. "If we launch a diversion, then strike Tenboro while security is thin, perhaps we can manage to take the viceroy's head."

Haruhiro and the others had returned to General Mogis along with Barbara. The reason they gave for her accompaniment was that it would be better for her to speak with him directly rather than to pass along secondhand information. More accurately, Barbara wanted to decide for herself just how much they should reveal to the general. From Barbara's perspective, there was a big difference between acting with knowledge of the general's character, and not.

Deep inside the Expeditionary Force's camp, General Mogis had a space with a table and chairs set up where he could hold a war council. As the dark of night encroached on the camp, General Mogis, three of his closest warriors, Neal the scout, Anthony, Haruhiro, Merry, and Barbara were all there. They were short a chair, however, so Haruhiro ended up standing.

"I want a map." The general looked at Barbara. "A detailed map. With all the escape holes drawn in. Can you prepare one?"

"That's possible." Barbara smiled. "We'd have to copy our map of Alterna and give it to you. It would take some time."

The general put his hands down on the table and gave her a sharp look. "Hand it over as-is."

Barbara's smile deepened. "That will not be possible."

"Why?" the general asked without missing a beat.

"The thing's a mess." Barbara licked her lips and let out a low chuckle. "I'm afraid, with the way it's drawn, only we can understand it."

"When we scouts draw maps, we have our own style," Neal interjected. "If you don't know how to read it, it's probably meaningless. The thieves in the frontier must use similar methods. I should be able to read it."

Barbara tut-tutted him teasingly. "No, you can't. We have our own ways of doing things in the frontier."

Neal shrugged. "Maybe you're right."

"Have the map ready in three days," the general demanded in a monotone. "I cannot wait any longer."

"Oh, my." Barbara was still smiling. "You don't like being kept in suspense, do you? But if you don't wait, what will you do?"

"Anyone who does not cooperate with our army will be deemed an obstacle."

"Forceful, aren't we? I don't mind that in a man."

"Clever women like you are a favorite of mine too. I always find myself wanting to devour them."

Was he serious, or was that a threat? Or maybe even a joke? Whatever it was, if the general could say that with a serious look on his face, it was safe to say, at the very least, he did not possess an average, ordinary sort of mind.

Although the way Barbara didn't back down was extraordinary too. "Well, I prefer to be the one doing the devouring. Now, let's assume I'm going to make you the map. How many people will be going into Alterna?"

"Fifty to one hundred at most. The rest will attack from outside."

"What will you do once you take Alterna?"

"That is nothing you need to be concerned about."

"We're surrounded by enemies, General. Just north of Alterna, there're hundreds of orcs in Deadhead Watching Keep."

"I am aware."

"The goblins and orcs aren't on friendly terms, but..." Anthony hesitantly said.

"The Kingdom of Arabakia wants Alterna." The general looked around at everyone. "The Expeditionary Force *must* take Alterna. That is the duty we have been tasked with."

There was no room for negotiation. No matter what anyone said, the general wasn't likely to change course.

Barbara looked up to the sky and sighed. She stroked her chin and thought for a moment, then glanced back at the general. "Making the map, bringing the soldiers into Alterna, and getting them in position will take ten days to prepare."

"Five days," said the general.

Barbara cocked her head to the side a little. "How does eight days sound?"

"Seven days."

"Can it be eight days, including this one, which is nearly over?"

"Very well."

"Then we'll prepare for eight days, including today, and act on the ninth day."

The general silently nodded.

"Well." Barbara gave him a sexy smile. "I think we might just barely make it in time."

"You seem like you'd be better suited to running a brothel than working as a thief," the general said emotionlessly.

"I think sleeping with good men and women suits me."

"For me," the general gave her a smile so faint it might not even have been there, "whether it's men or women, barbarians, beasts, or monsters, trampling them is what suits me best."

Jin Mogis was as inscrutable as ever. But his claim to enjoy trampling things and stomping them into the ground might have been true.

Whatever the case, the discussion was at an end. In nine days, they would carry out the operation to retake Alterna. Though it wasn't the ten days that Barbara had originally asked for, it was a fair amount of time to work with.

When Barbara went back to Alterna to prepare the map, Neal was sent to accompany her. They said it was to help with the work, but he was basically there to monitor her.

Haruhiro and Merry headed to the tent where their comrades were waiting. They had a mountain of things to talk about, but Neal wasn't the only scout around. People working for General Mogis or Neal might be listening in, so they had to be careful when sharing information. They didn't have a lot of time, but they had enough. There was no need to rush.

The next day, the general made an announcement to the whole army. "Eight days from now, our Expeditionary Force will launch a glorious operation critical to our goal. To that end, I will be recruiting a suicide squad to go on a dangerous mission. Until fifty men volunteer, each day, I will take one person who has broken regulations and personally execute them."

It was an abnormal, even crazy announcement. Haruhiro was sure the general was serious, but most of the soldiers didn't seem to be taking it that way. There were no volunteers on the first day.

Just after the sun set, the general looked around the camp. Though the soldiers feared the general, a good number of them were grinning or lying about as if they didn't care.

The general suddenly stopped and ordered one soldier who was sitting on the ground looking away from him to stand. The man didn't hesitate and was on his feet fairly quickly. He was a young soldier, probably around twenty years old.

"What is it?" the soldier asked.

"Have you ever broken regulations?"

"No, I don't think so."

"Is that true?"

"I have not."

"Who is your superior officer?" The general looked around.

The old soldier who was sitting nearby stood up. "I am," he said.

"Has he broken regulations?" the general asked.

"I don't believe he's done anything in particular," the old soldier responded.

"Then were you given orders that said you could sit here?"

"No," the old soldier looked uneasy. "We were not."

"That's right. I didn't order you to sit. Doing things I didn't order you to is against regulations."

The general suddenly drew his sword and decapitated the young soldier. His head rolled, and his body slumped to the ground. The camp fell silent.

The general calmly wiped the blood from his sword using his black fur cloak, then returned it to its scabbard. "Clean this up," he ordered the old soldier.

"Y-yes, sir!" The old soldier nodded repeatedly.

"Now, then." The general looked around at the rest. "Is there anyone in this Expeditionary Force who has not violated regulations? I wonder how many more I will have to kill. What a bother."

And so, the soldiers were left with a dilemma. Jin Mogis had specifically called the group he was recruiting a suicide squad. The mission was sure to be harsh. They had to be prepared to die in the battle to come, because they surely would. Though not all of the volunteers were guaranteed to die, there was a high likelihood that any or all of them might.

If they volunteered, they might die during the mission, but they wouldn't be executed for violating regulations. In addition, if the number of volunteers reached fifty, no one would be cut down by the general until the operation started. However, if there were a thousand troops in the Expeditionary Force, there was a one in a thousand chance they might be executed by the general tomorrow. If they weren't exceptionally unlucky, they weren't going to win—no, in this case, perhaps lose was the better word—this particular lottery.

The soldiers thought about it on their own, talked with their friends, told those they didn't get along with to volunteer, fought, mediated, loudly criticized others, got into fistfights, and spent the night without sleeping.

Haruhiro and his group probably wouldn't be executed, but the murderous air in the camp was uncomfortable. In the middle of the night, Anthony came to visit them as they talked in secret, no more able to get to sleep than the soldiers.

"I told you, didn't I? The general is no ordinary man. Even knowing that, I was waiting to see how he would get this army to fight, but...I never expected that."

"Think he'll get fifty?" Kuzaku asked in a tone laced with disgust.

"I wonder," Anthony mumbled, not giving a proper answer, then sat down next to Kuzaku. Kuzaku was clearly annoyed with him.

It seemed, for Anthony, the most important thing about another person was whether they were a mainlander or from the frontier. Haruhiro and his group were people of the frontier, so Anthony felt closer to them than to the mainlanders.

"The situation in the mainland that the general told me about..." Anthony said in a low voice. "Do you think it's all true?"

"We couldn't possibly say." Setora didn't mince words.

Anthony hung his head. "I guess not."

"Me, I'm just gonna do what I have to, y'know?" Kuzaku said, trying to smooth things over.

"Those are exactly the words I'd expect from someone without a thought in his head." Setora scoffed.

"You're always so quick to say things like that, Setora-san."

"You guys have got it good," Anthony said all of a sudden. "I'm jealous."

Haruhiro wasn't sure what he was jealous of, but if Anthony learned that all of them but Merry had lost their memories, would he still feel the same way? Maybe he'd actually feel even more envious.

But the more things you cared about enough to fear losing them, the harder it was to act.

Since returning to Alterna, Haruhiro hadn't had a proper conversation with Shihoru. She seemed kind of cold, like she was avoiding him.

Grimgar of Fantasy and Ash

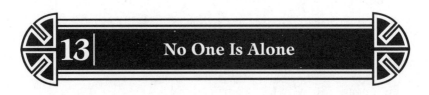

13 | No One Is Alone

BARBARA WAS STANDING about ten meters ahead, directly in front of Haruhiro. They were in the forest, but there were no trees obstructing the line of sight between them. The ground was mostly flat too. Barbara looked like she might be smiling faintly, but she was close to expressionless.

Whenever a person or an animal was about to make a move, there were signs beforehand: a tension in the muscles, tendons, and even the skin, phenomena which told you that they were about to take action. Haruhiro couldn't detect any of that in Barbara.

Barbara wore a highly revealing outfit, and her physique and face were awfully sexy, so she stood out like a sore thumb. Despite that, for some reason, she had oddly little sense of presence. She just stood there like a Barbara-shaped plant. It was hard to imagine she was even alive.

Haruhiro blinked. It was unintentional. In that instant, there was a sound to his right. While he was distracted by the noise,

Barbara disappeared. A person had vanished in an instant. Was that even possible?

It was. Haruhiro knew the trick. His eyes were closed only momentarily when he blinked. It was impossible to hide in that time, but it was possible to throw something to make noise. Naturally, if there was a noise, he would reflexively focus on it. At that point, Barbara had gained the time she needed to disappear.

His pulse was elevated, and blood rushed to his head. *Damn. She got me.*

He couldn't help but panic, but if he lost his head, he'd be doing just what Barbara wanted. He took a breath, straightened out the knees he had bent at some point, and loosened up his tense shoulders and arms.

Of course that would happen. He accepted it. Barbara was a level or two above him in ability, so it was entirely to be expected.

Where was she lurking now? It was important to try to predict her. But he couldn't let his predictions bind or mislead him.

Haruhiro kept his eyes focused on one point, scanning a wide area around him. He perked up his ears. Was there another sound, one hidden in the rustling of leaves, the sound of insects, the chirping of birds? His own breathing got in the way. He tried to make his breaths as gentle as possible.

Going all out, he tried closing his eyes. Time went by, but he was unable to pick up on anything. No, that wasn't entirely true. Haruhiro was gradually learning to sense the entire forest around him.

He opened his eyes. He could even feel the places he couldn't see, now. Something felt off ahead of him, to the left. There was a tree about seven meters from Haruhiro, a chinquapin, or something like that.

Oh, he thought. *There, that has to be it.* He was immediately convinced as prediction turned to certainty. Having a need to confirm it for himself, he walked around to the other side of the tree. She wasn't there.

He'd considered this possibility. It would be easy for Barbara to work against Haruhiro's assumptions. She would be able to leave a trace of herself here somehow, then secretly move elsewhere.

Where was she now? Very close.

Haruhiro tried to turn. No. She wasn't behind him.

He jumped back, and something fell from the tree. She had been above, not behind.

"You got it."

The moment Barbara landed, she drew her dagger and came at him. Haruhiro pulled out his own dagger, but Barbara smoothly avoided his attempts to parry her. Haruhiro immediately went on the counterattack, but was that his choice, or was he forced into it? No matter what angle he attacked from, Barbara slipped away. He couldn't catch her.

What is this?

The moment he sensed he had no way to attack her, their roles as attacker and defender switched. Barbara went on the offensive. The arc of her dagger bent and twisted, making it hard to see, and she frequently closed or opened the gap between them, trying to sweep his leg, or using her free hand to shove his arm. It was seriously hard to deal with.

Though he was having difficulty, he tried whatever technique he could—or felt like he might be able to pull off—one after another. However, Barbara apparently saw through everything he tried. She read his every move. She could probably even hear the beating of his heart.

There was so little he could do about her, it was comical.

Haruhiro's breathing quickened, his movements dulled, and finally his right hand, which held the dagger, was put in a joint lock. He let go and was thrown, then instantly pressed to the ground.

"Surrender?" Barbara asked. She had him in a side-control hold.

"I give. It hurts."

"You sure it doesn't actually feel good?"

"No, it just hurts..."

"Even without your memories, you're the same as ever, huh?" Barbara released Haruhiro but didn't stand. She sat on the ground with one knee raised.

Following her example, Haruhiro sat up and crossed his legs. "How am I doing?"

"Your instincts are coming back, aren't they? It seemed like your body remembered me."

Haruhiro put on a strained smile. He wasn't sure about the way she'd phrased that, but the thief techniques Barbara had drilled into him were certainly still there. They hadn't vanished.

Before dawn tomorrow, the Expeditionary Force would launch the operation to retake Alterna. Multiple holes connected Alterna to the outside. Those holes were interconnected in a few places.

Already, a little over eighty soldiers—including the fifty-four in the suicide squad—hid beneath the dread knights' guild in West Town, the warriors' guild in the southern district, and the Temple of Lumiaris in the northern district.

There had been forty-eight volunteers for the suicide squad on day two, and when the general began looking for someone to execute for violating military protocol, six more rapidly raised their hands. That made for more volunteers than needed, but the general said, "If you're so eager to die, I'll let you," and added all six of them to the squad for a total of fifty-four. But that was just another fond memory now.

To give a rough rundown of the plan, the main Expeditionary Force, led by General Mogis, would attack Alterna's south gate. When the goblins began defending, the fifty-four-member suicide squad would move. Their mission was to open Alterna's south gate from the inside. Even if they couldn't open it, the fact that there would be humans inside Alterna trying to open the gate was meaningful in and of itself.

If they were attacked from both sides—within and without— the goblins were bound to panic. Using that confusion, a group composed of people the general trusted, along with Anthony Justeen and his subordinates, as well as Haruhiro's group, would storm Tenboro Tower and strike down Viceroy Bogg.

Their group had been given a rather important job. Kuzaku could fight as he was. Setora could manage, too, if she had a weapon. Plus, she had Kiichi. Shihoru had learned to use her Dark magic. Merry, it went without saying, would have no problems.

Would Haruhiro be all right, in the end? He wasn't without misgivings, but Barbara had certified his skills while retraining him.

"Okay, so, I guess we can say I pass?" Haruhiro asked his teacher.

"Old Cat."

"Yes?"

Barbara wrapped her arm around Haruhiro's head and mussed his hair.

"Wh-what are you doing?"

"You've really grown since I last saw you, huh?"

"Do you think? I don't remember it, so I couldn't say one way or the other."

"But you held back because you were facing me, right?"

"That wasn't my intent. I sure wasn't doing well enough that I could afford to..."

"It was a bad match-up. You weren't trying to kill me, right?"

"Huh? But...isn't that obvious?"

"It's not about whether you have the balls to do it," Barbara said, reaching down to try and squeeze his actual balls.

Haruhiro stopped her at the last second. "Whoa, you don't have to grab them, right?!"

"Nah," Barbara smiled, then hugged Haruhiro's head. He was surprised, of course, but he couldn't resist. "Listen, Old Cat. The important thing is to set an appropriate goal."

Barbara rubbed Haruhiro all over, kissed him on the forehead, and gave him an intimate lesson.

"Work backwards from that goal to formulate a plan. Obviously, things will diverge from expectations, so you need to stay flexible. But if you start with the wrong goal, any strategy will be meaningless. If you're facing me, even in practice, you've got to kill me. That has to be where you set your goal. Even if you don't ultimately do it. Do you get it?"

"Yes, Sensei."

Haruhiro felt incredibly embarrassed, and he wanted to run away, but for some reason he didn't push Barbara off of him. He couldn't defy her. Was that something his body had learned?

"You're just running straight ahead with no idea where you're going. There's no way to win like that. In fact, you were never convinced you needed to, I'll bet. You lost because you were meant to."

Maybe, even though this was embarrassing, he actually found it more comfortable.

"Here's the thing, Old Cat. You've got a wide perspective, and you don't scare easily. Your thinking's only average, though. You don't overestimate yourself, and you've got the stubbornness to work through things a little at a time. Those parts of you won't change, even if you don't remember them. You're not the type who can do things if he tries. You're the type that tries until he can

do things. That's why, right now, it's good that there are things you can't do. Because someday you're going to be able to do them."

Haruhiro couldn't help but think, *Before I lost my memories, I was a pretty lucky guy.*

Haruhiro, who Barbara said hadn't seemed likely to live long when she first met him, had survived to this day. He must have done his best, in his own way. Or, at the very least, he'd tried to. But more than anything, it had to be thanks to his comrades and his teacher. If it weren't for them, Haruhiro would long since have died, wouldn't he?

He didn't know what would happen tomorrow, but the outlook wasn't exactly bright.

Barbara returned to Alterna with Neal, her watcher. Meanwhile, Haruhiro and the Tenboro Tower raid squad would set out when the sun set. He was supposed to take a nap until then.

Haruhiro lay down inside the tent, but he couldn't get to sleep. Kuzaku was snoring next to him. Even though Kuzaku had said, *"There's no way I could sleep,"* he was out in an instant. Haruhiro seriously envied that part of Kuzaku.

He'd known it was going to be like this, but he couldn't help it. There was no way he could sleep. Haruhiro gave up and left the tent.

Merry and Shihoru were sitting next to each other. The two of them looked at Haruhiro.

"Haru."

"Haruhiro-kun."

No, they weren't next to each other. There was about a meter between them. They weren't facing each other, but they weren't parallel either. They were at a bit of an angle, but not one where their eyes met, and it didn't seem like they'd been talking.

"Yeah..." Haruhiro nodded vaguely. He didn't know what to do. The distance between them was awkward. It would be weird to sit between them. Not impossible, but a tight fit. *Yeah, no,* Haruhiro thought. That wasn't an option.

He agonized over it for a moment, then sat down so that the three of them formed an equilateral triangle.

He immediately regretted it. No matter what he did, the other two were constantly looking at him. It was awkward, but it would be weird to move now, so he'd just have to live with it.

"Erm...where's Setora?" he asked, then regretted it again.

"Sleeping with Kiichi," Merry answered.

"Oh, yeah?" Haruhiro said, adding an, "Of course she is," under his breath, and rubbed the point between his eyes. He should have chosen a topic it was easier to build a conversation off of.

"It..." Shihoru opened her mouth.

"Huh?" Haruhiro said.

Shihoru hung her head. "It's tomorrow, huh? It's finally happening..."

"Ohh, uh. Yeah," Haruhiro hurriedly replied. Shihoru had gone out of her way to give him an opening, so he wanted to make something of it. "Well, we've just been going with the flow. But I have to wonder if...I dunno, wasn't there a way to handle things that would have been less dangerous for everyone?"

"I don't think it's your fault, Haru," said Merry.

"M-me either!" Shihoru vigorously agreed. "I don't think it is either. You've really, really...been trying hard, for all of us..."

It had felt like Shihoru was avoiding him, but maybe he'd just been imagining it. Haruhiro was relieved. "Nah, when you say I'm doing it for everyone, it makes me sound like I'm some great guy, but it's nothing that impressive. Really. Yeah..."

Merry smiled. "You were always like that, Haru."

Shihoru glanced sideways at Merry, then immediately looked down. Merry looked at Shihoru, lowered her eyes, and bit her lip, but just a little. After that, the two of them were quiet.

Why? Huh? Huh? Huh? Why would they get quiet all of a sudden there? Haruhiro had no idea.

This sort of thing troubled him, and it was tough, so he wanted to make things better. If there was a problem to fix, he wanted to fix it. He would have liked to talk it over, but he wasn't sure. Much as he'd have liked to propose listening to their unvarnished opinions, then having a constructive debate over whatever the issue was, the silence dragged on without him being able to do anything about it.

In the end, Haruhiro finally managed to open his mouth. "L-Let's do our best."

When he did, the two of them gulped, then looked at him. They both looked like they were expecting something.

I've got nothing, though? They could expect all they wanted, but nothing would be forthcoming. "Tomorrow, let's all...work together..." Adding that was the best he could manage.

"Yes," Merry nodded. "Of course."

Shihoru smiled just a little. Or she tried to, at least. "Okay."

Before sundown, Kuzaku, Setora, and Kiichi came out of the tent.

"Whew, I know I said I couldn't, but I was pretty soundly asleep there, huh?"

"I was just resting my eyes, though."

"Nyaa."

"Setora-san, really, is there some reason you need to act tough like that?"

"I am not acting tough. I am merely stating the facts."

"You can be like this sometimes, huh, Setora-san?"

"Be like what?"

The Tenboro Tower raid team was commanded by Dylan Stone—a close associate of General Mogis—and Anthony Justeen as the second-in-command. Together with five warriors from the Frontier Army Warrior Regiment who were Anthony's subordinates, eight soldiers from the Expeditionary Force, and Haruhiro's group of five, plus Kiichi, they had a total of twenty people and one nyaa.

Commander Dylan was a gloomy forty-something with a big nose and bushy beard. As you could tell from the black fur cloak he wore—the same as the general's—he was from the Black Hounds too. He was always cursing people and things. He told them to "go die" a lot.

Incidentally, all the soldiers from the Expeditionary Force were also wearing black fur cloaks. It seemed safe to assume from the general's selection that he had filled the Tenboro Tower raid team with people he trusted.

The raid team set out as soon as the sun went down, entered Alterna through a secret tunnel in the middle of the night, and joined up with Neal the scout in the dread knights' guild. Barbara-sensei, who Neal had been watching all this time, was supposed to be staking out Tenboro Tower around now.

The dread knights' guild was also where twenty members of the suicide squad were standing by. When the main body of the Expeditionary Force led by General Mogis attacked, the suicide squad would have to charge toward Alterna's south gate.

Commander Dylan of the raid team offered the suicide squad some words of encouragement. "If you think of it like you're going to die anyway, then dying's no big deal. In the unlikely event you survive, you got lucky. We only die once, and everyone's got to eventually. So go die, you absolute bastards."

Commander Dylan knew every one of the members of the suicide squad, so in his own way, he was probably trying to motivate them. It was hard to imagine any of them felt encouraged by his words, though. If anything, they looked like they had less life in them than before.

Commander Dylan was a man of few words, but when he did speak, he always demotivated those around him. Even when he didn't, he had this air that was exhausting on its own, so nobody wanted to be too close to him.

Haruhiro and Neal went aboveground to check on the situation. When the main body of the Expeditionary Force attacked the south gate, they had to alert the suicide squad. It was quiet, with nobody—or rather, no goblin—in sight in predawn Alterna. The two of them left West Town, then climbed up the walls to the roof of what used to be the volunteer soldier lodging house. Haruhiro had apparently lived in that lodging house once upon a time, but he didn't remember it at all.

"This is a disaster," Neal whispered to Haruhiro with a low laugh. "That bastard Dylan is the reaper himself. Lots of people get killed in any squad he leads. He's the only one guaranteed to survive."

"Won't you be part of the raid too?"

"As if. I'm a scout. I have to watch your exploits from afar, then report back to the general."

"Oh, is that right?"

"Let me tell you something. Dylan Stone is an inhuman monster who's good at using others as his shields. He doesn't care if the rest of you survive or not. The general likes guys like him."

"It looks like the general trusts you, though."

"Trusts me?" Neal tried to put an overly friendly arm around Haruhiro's shoulder. When Haruhiro dodged, Neal gave him an exaggerated frown. "The general doesn't trust anybody. He's only looking to see who's willing to wag their tail and do as he says. I won't betray the general. I follow orders because it works to my benefit."

To turn that around, if it wasn't to Neal's benefit, he wouldn't follow orders and wouldn't hesitate to betray the man.

The leader was bad and so were his followers. But Haruhiro's group had to risk their lives on a big mission with these people. Worse, they'd been integrated into the larger group. They were all in the same boat now. Haruhiro hated it, but he had no choice.

It was still a while before sunrise, but the eastern sky was brightening.

"It'll be any moment now," Neal said with a sniff. "This is the day when we meet our destiny."

It was a pretentious way to put it, but then, it might not have been an exaggeration.

They heard muddled cries from the south. The clanging of gongs followed.

"Go." Neal slapped Haruhiro on the back. "And don't you dare die."

Haruhiro hadn't expected Neal to say that. He was a little surprised, but when he looked, Neal was smirking. None of General Mogis's subordinates were good people. "You too, Neal," Haruhiro said, though he didn't mean it, then hurried down from the roof of the lodging house.

He jumped into an alley and ran. The noise was nothing like before, when Haruhiro and his group were chased off after approaching Alterna. There were gongs and bells ringing everywhere, and goblins were hollering wildly. The goblins that had been sleeping inside the buildings must have jumped up and rushed outside. The street was already full of them.

Haruhiro nearly ran into goblins a number of times, but maybe because he had Barbara's map committed to memory, he managed to use the back streets to reach the dread knights' guild.

When Commander Dylan heard Haruhiro's report, he ordered everyone up into the ruined house that was the aboveground portion of the guild. Within the house were narrow corridors and a number of small rooms.

"Okay, it's a good day to die. So go die, you bastards."

Commander Dylan practically chased the suicide squad out of the building, then entered a room that could hold five people at most and sat down on a poorly made chair that looked like a footstool.

"What about us?" Haruhiro asked from outside the small room.

"Stand by," Commander Dylan ordered, crossing his arms and closing his eyes.

Haruhiro gathered his comrades in another room, near the exit to the ruined house, next to the room where Anthony and his men waited. But this room was cramped too.

"Ahh..." When Kuzaku stretched, his hand nearly touched Setora.

"Hey," Setora glared at him. Kiichi hissed a warning too.

Kuzaku chuckled and said, "Sorry. I'm feeling tense," then yawned.

"What is with this guy?" Setora asked in exasperation.

"It seems when he gets tense, he starts feeling sleepy, or yawns," Merry tried to explain.

"Yeah, that's it," Kuzaku said, acting a bit cocky. "That's so it. That has to be what it is."

Shihoru looked up, taking large breaths, in and out, repeatedly.

"You okay?" Haruhiro asked.

Shihoru turned to Haruhiro and gave him a slightly sheepish smile. "Because everyone's here."

"Yeah," was all he could summon. It made Haruhiro ask himself, *Couldn't you say more than that? Do I respond with "yeah" a bit too often? Wouldn't "Yeah, that's right," be better? I guess they're the same, huh? Yeah, they're the same.*

He felt a little fuzzy. He wasn't like Kuzaku, but he might have been feeling tense. No, of course he was tense. If he thought he was calm, that was nothing but an illusion.

"Um...Merry?" Shihoru said.

Merry seemed caught by surprise, and her eyes widened. "Huh?"

The two of them looked at each other. That's when it hit Haruhiro that he really was feeling tense. Or rather, it hit him what this weird feeling of tension was: like he was in a powder keg.

Shihoru bowed her head. "Please."

Merry couldn't seem to figure out what her intentions were and was unable to say whatever it was she wanted to, because her mouth bobbed open and shut.

Shihoru raised her head, then tried to put on a smile. Her effort was visible, but she still ended up with a face that looked like she was about to cry.

Merry burst out laughing, covered her mouth, burst out laughing again, then looked down. "Sorry."

Shihoru shook her head. "No, I'm the one who should be sorry."

There seemed to be a peace between Merry and Shihoru, but what was even going on here? Haruhiro looked to Setora, hoping she'd save him.

Setora hugged Kiichi and committed herself to acting like she didn't know what was up.

"Right on!" Kuzaku said to Haruhiro with a beaming smile and gave him a thumbs-up.

What's supposed to be "right on"? Haruhiro might have asked him, but right then, there was a sound like someone trying to open the door to the ruined house.

"There's been movement at Tenboro Tower! Viceroy Bogg's...!"

It was Barbara's voice. Haruhiro readied to rush out of the room.

"Wait!" Merry stopped him. She pressed her fingers to her forehead and made the sign of the hexagram. "O Light, may Lumiaris's divine protection be upon you... Protection."

A shining hexagram appeared on the group's left wrists.

Merry continued chanting another prayer. "Assist."

Two more hexagrams of different colors lit up on their wrists.

Kuzaku bounced up and laughed. "I feel so light."

Protection was a light magic spell that boosted their athletic abilities and natural healing, even if it wasn't massively. Assist boosted all their resistances.

"Thanks," Haruhiro said to Merry.

Merry shook her head. "If the effect runs out, I'll recast it. I'll do my best to notice ahead of time, but if the hexagram disappears, tell me."

Haruhiro nodded, then looked at his comrades. "Let's go."

Grimgar
of
Fantasy and Ash

14 | The Road to an Old Cat

WHEN HE HEARD Barbara's urgent report, Commander Dylan Stone gave the order at once. "We're heading out, you bastards!"

The raid team hurriedly left the dread knights' guild. Second-in-Command Anthony, who knew the area, was ordered to lead the way. His subordinates, Haruhiro's group, and Commander Dylan's black-cloaked soldiers followed him.

Barbara ran alongside Haruhiro. "I didn't expect Viceroy Bogg to come out of Tenboro Tower for us! This is a one-in-a-million chance!"

Right after they left the dread knights' guild, a goblin found them. It ran away, hollering something.

"Do we chase it?!" Anthony shouted.

"You stupid bastard!" Dylan bellowed from behind. "Let that insignificant little bastard go, and keep moving!"

To Commander Dylan, allies and enemies were both bastards. Kuzaku muttered something like, "You're the biggest bastard here," and, honestly, Haruhiro agreed.

Regardless, the raid team ignored the goblin and pressed forward.

According to Barbara, not long after the main force began their attack, four or five of the Hundred had come out of Tenboro Tower and led a few dozen goblins toward the south gate. After that, a goblin that looked like a messenger rushed into Tenboro Tower. When it did, Viceroy Bogg appeared, leading about ten of the Hundred. The Hundred took off in all directions while Viceroy Bogg remained alone in the plaza.

Barbara's read on the situation was that Viceroy Bogg was gathering the elite fighters before personally heading to the south gate.

Tenboro Tower was a reasonably tall building, but only the first and second floor, which had the entrance hall and reception hall, were particularly wide. Everything above that was spiral staircases, hallways, and small rooms. It was designed to be defensible if it came to it.

The plan had called for the raid team to break into Tenboro Tower and slay Viceroy Bogg, but if they could catch him outside, nothing was better than that. However, being outside came with its own dangers. The goblins had an overwhelming numerical advantage. Despite that, inside a building or another tight space, they wouldn't end up in an extreme situation, like twenty people versus a thousand of these animals. But outside, in the worst-case scenario, goblins might press in on them from all directions.

When they left West Town and entered the southern district, a meager force of ten goblins blocked their way.

"We're charging!" Anthony shouted. "Warriors of the frontier, show them your pride!"

Anthony and his five warriors tore into the goblin line without hesitation.

Was it an exaggeration to say they swept the goblins away? When Anthony and his men clashed with the enemy and swung their swords, four or five of the goblins were cut down or sent flying. The goblins that were not slain lost their balance and fled in the blink of an eye.

"Hey, those guys're strong!" Kuzaku said cheerfully.

"The enemy is just weak," Barbara chuckled. "Old Cat, I'm going to circle around, check the situation, and come back."

"Yes, Sensei!"

"Good response." Barbara blew him a kiss as she left the raid team.

They pushed farther and farther forward, heading for the plaza in front of Tenboro Tower.

"Anthony-san!" Haruhiro raised his voice.

"What?!" Anthony didn't turn back.

"Slow down a little! You're going too fast! We're already winded!"

"Right! Got it!"

"Don't tell him things you don't need to, you bastard!" Dylan shouted at him, but he didn't say anything more than that, so Haruhiro didn't care.

Am I calm now? I don't think I'm panicking. I can see what's going on around me pretty well. Though I may just be imagining that.

No, it wasn't that he could see it, it was that he was looking. Barbara had said he had a wide field of vision, but Haruhiro was turning his head without realizing it himself, always surveying the surrounding area. It was a habit he'd developed. Maybe thanks to that, Haruhiro was the first to spot the squad of goblins that were closing in on the raid team.

There were only fifteen or so, but they all carried round shields and spears. It wasn't just their equipment that was unified, though. They moved in an organized fashion.

Behind us! Haruhiro tried to yell. There was another goblin on the roof of a two-floor building that faced the street, and he had just pulled a reddish sword. One of the Hundred, huh? Haruhiro made a snap decision.

"Shihoru!" Haruhiro pointed to the Hundred on the roof.

Shihoru stopped and turned both palms toward the Hundred. "Dark!"

Dark appeared, as if pushing open an invisible door, the black threads intertwining, weaving into a humanoid form. Dark let out a bizarre *nshooooooo* sound and flew toward the Hundred. The goblin cried out in shock and tried to cut Dark with its sword. But Dark slipped around the blade and got behind his target. The Hundred turned, looking for Dark. At that point, Dark was already inside it.

"Commander Dylan!" Haruhiro shouted. "The enemy is coming from behind!"

"The little bastards!" Commander Dylan spat. "I'll kill them all!"

"Ngh!" One of Anthony's men went down.

He'd been hit by an arrow—no, a bolt. Another five or six goblins with crossbows were on a different roof than the Hundred. They had fired a volley, and one or two of the bolts had struck Anthony's subordinate.

"I'll treat him!" Merry shouted, rushing over.

It looked like Commander Dylan could handle the ones behind. Meanwhile, the Hundred flailed its red sword as Dark toyed with it, but the creature realized it wasn't getting anywhere and threw itself down from the roof.

"Anthony! Kuzaku!" Haruhiro shouted, accidentally addressing Anthony without an honorific.

When the Hundred that had dropped onto the road brandished its red sword and hollered, goblins rushed out of alleyways. Anthony and his men let out a war cry and charged. Kuzaku launched a fierce assault on the Hundred. Merry tried to get Anthony's injured man back up.

"Setora, protect Merry!"

"Right!"

"Shihoru, behind me!"

"Okay!"

The goblin crossbow team was reloading. Before Haruhiro could even give the order, Shihoru sent Dark after them.

A goblin got past Anthony and his men and came toward them with a spear. Shihoru was behind Haruhiro. He couldn't back away.

The spear's tip aimed for Haruhiro's solar plexus. At the last possible moment, he turned sideways, putting his left side forward. If he had only dodged, the spear would have threatened Shihoru instead. That's why Haruhiro pushed the spear's shaft to the side using his hand. The goblin wore a helmet that completely covered its head, and the visor only had the thinnest of openings. It didn't look like it provided good visibility or hearing, but it was a solid helmet. It also had chainmail armor and even a breast plate.

Haruhiro got up close. When the goblin faltered, he stomped hard on its right foot. Even though it had a helmet and armor, the goblin was still barefoot. On its lower half, it only wore some kind of leather pants. Haruhiro buried his dagger in the goblin's right thigh, just above the knee. It shrieked and threw its head back in pain.

He grabbed the goblin by the jaw with his left hand and twisted as he pushed it to the ground. He got on top of it, and using the weight of both knees, he pushed down on the goblin's jaw even harder.

As the goblin cried out and desperately resisted, Haruhiro flipped up the visor on its helm. He saw the goblin's face through the opening. He took his dagger, holding it in his right hand with a backhand grip, and plunged it into the goblin's left eye. He gave it a deep, deep thrust and twisted.

The goblin let out a wretched cry and fell limp.

Before Haruhiro could think *That finished it,* he'd already jumped away from the goblin.

"Keep going!" Commander Dylan shouted.

"But they know we're here!" Haruhiro yelled back. "The Hundred are coming to stop us!"

"You think we can call off the attack now, you bastard?! We're going to carry out the mission, even if everyone dies in the process!"

Haruhiro couldn't help but think, *You say that, but I bet you're planning to survive on your own. You're the real bastard here.*

"I'm not saying to call it off! But if we just charge in with no plan—"

"Yahhhhhhhhh...!" Kuzaku slashed the Hundred.

"The losses we'll take will—" Haruhiro was speechless.

The goblins were panicking.

"Don't let the little bastards stop you!" Commander Dylan spurred them on. "We only need to take that one bastard's head! Onward, you bastards, onward!"

"Which bastard, you bastard?!" Anthony shouted back reflexively. He swung his sword and kept going. "We're going, raid team! After me!"

The man Merry had been healing got up and followed Anthony.

Everything was happening so fast, Haruhiro couldn't keep up. Okay, no, that wasn't true. Even without telling himself to change gears, he was already going with the flow. There was something to what Commander Dylan was saying, crude though he might be. For the raid team, speed was of the utmost importance.

"Shihoru! Setora! Merry! Kuzaku! Kiichi!" Haruhiro thought for a moment, but came up blank. He simply shouted, "Let's go!"

"'Kay!"

"Right!"

"Yes!"

"Nyaa!"

"Okay!"

They didn't have time to think about pacing themselves now. *Faster. Faster.* They had to go as fast as they could without leaving people behind. If they didn't, they might get surrounded. Even if they did, goblins would still come at them. Commander Dylan said to ignore the goblins, but there were times when, if they didn't shove goblins aside or scatter them, there was no way forward.

Haruhiro ran, looked, listened, and made decisions, giving orders to Kuzaku and Setora, issuing warnings to Anthony, and kicking goblins to the ground. His lungs and throat ached. Shihoru looked like she was having a hard time. She was doing everything she could to keep up.

"To the plaza!" Anthony shouted.

The road was curved and opened up ahead of them.

What about Barbara-sensei? Haruhiro thought all of a sudden. *What's taking her? She said she'd go on ahead and take a look. No, that wasn't it. She wasn't just going to take a look; she was going to check the situation and come back.*

The raid team finally entered the plaza.

Before, it had been a wide-open space with nothing but cobblestone. Not now. There were these huge, ominous *things* made with wood and stone, leather and cloth, metal parts, bone or

something, and this weird blackish paint Haruhiro couldn't identify. Were they towers? Huts? Or maybe platforms? Whatever
they were, they had been built all over. But toward the center,
near Tenboro Tower, the space had been deliberately left open.
That area was still being used as a plaza, or maybe a road.

Even from a distance, Haruhiro spotted a group of goblins
on that road, heading toward Tenboro Tower. It was hard to tell
how many there were with all the massive objects in the way. It
wasn't more than a hundred, but there were still thirty to forty.
They were marching with their spears together, so it was easy to
recognize them from a distance and to eyeball their number.

It looked like there was something on the tips of their spears.

"Is that it?!" Anthony shouted, knocking down a goblin that
lunged at him from the shadow of one of the objects.

"You bastards! Here is where you die!" Commander Dylan
bellowed. What he probably wanted to say was that the thing
they were looking at was probably Viceroy Bogg's unit, and the
raid team needed to eliminate them no matter what.

These were goblins, but it was possible there were multiple
Hundreds in the group. Viceroy Bogg was definitely going to be a
veteran too. On top of that, they were outnumbered. It wasn't going to be easy. In fact, it was going to be incredibly difficult. They
had to launch an ambush, then take Viceroy Bogg's head in the
chaos, and do it as quickly as possible. Nothing else would work.

Anthony didn't head straight for Viceroy Bogg; he was
instead following a course that brought them close to Tenboro
Tower. One of Anthony's subordinates ran into one of the massive

objects and fell over, but no one helped him up. Haruhiro kept running. The man would catch up on his own at some point, surely.

They'd gotten pretty close to Viceroy Bogg's spear team. What was on those spears? Why did it bother Haruhiro so much?

He couldn't see the spears clearly, so he couldn't say for certain, but from the very beginning he'd thought it might be a certain something. Despite that, he didn't think too deeply about it.

It wasn't that he tried not to think about it so much as he didn't have the time to think about anything. More than that, he didn't *want* to think.

Still, now that they were so close, he couldn't avert his eyes from the fact that on the tips of those bloodstained spears were the severed torso and limbs of an animal. It wasn't every spear. Out of the thirty to forty spears, they were on less than half. Maybe ten at most.

Would the goblins go out of their way to hunt wild animals just to hoist them on their spears at a time like this? Not likely. Then were those parts from their own kind? It wasn't unimaginable that the viceroy might have ordered that any goblin that disobeyed orders be executed, but that probably wasn't it.

Those parts were human, weren't they?

In other words, Haruhiro had suspected from the beginning that the goblins were hoisting the dismembered body of a human being on their spears.

But there were no humans in Alterna, or there shouldn't have been. There were vanishingly few, but it wasn't like there were absolutely none. Haruhiro and the raid team were all humans heading for Viceroy Bogg at this very moment, after all.

Though, if those remains weren't from someone on the raid team, the alternative explanations were severely limited.

Barbara had said, *"I'm going to circle around, check the situation, and come back."*

She still wasn't back yet.

Viceroy Bogg's spear squadron came to a stop. Had they noticed the raid team?

The squadron was on the road on the other side of the massive object in front of Anthony. The raid team raced around the object and into the road.

Haruhiro jumped out, too, going into a crouch. Anthony and his men were already fighting the spear team. The goblins didn't thrust with their spears, they swung them downwards, trying to clobber Anthony and his men. The men blocked the spears with swords and helmets, trying to push forward.

One of the objects impaled on a spear came loose and went flying.

It was a human arm. A right arm. There was a left arm too. Legs as well. Right. And left. The torso was cut into multiple pieces, the innards spilling out of it. And the head landed at Haruhiro's feet, rolling.

It was long-haired. Female. Haruhiro looked at her. Checking her face. He couldn't help himself.

"Haruhiro?!" Kuzaku pushed him to the ground.

Why did he do that? Haruhiro didn't think about it. On the cobblestones, right in front of where Haruhiro had landed, *she* was there.

Her right eye was closed, her left slightly open. Her lips just parted. Her right cheek was pressed to the cobbles. Because of that, her whole face sagged to the right side. Her face bore several cuts. It was filthy with blood.

This was nothing like the person who had said, *"Good response,"* and blown him a kiss.

In a way, it was. But this thing wasn't her. It had long since ceased functioning as a living being, so even if it had once been a part of Barbara, it was Barbara no longer.

Still, Haruhiro was intensely shaken by a feeling that he couldn't just leave it like this. On the other hand, he was well aware that he didn't have time to worry about it.

If Barbara were still alive, she would've scolded him. *"Hey, what are you doing, Old Cat?"*

But Haruhiro's teacher would never scold him again.

If he hadn't lost his memories, he would have felt an even stronger connection with her. If he had more memories with his teacher, this would have been even harder to take, and he might not have been able to stand it.

Haruhiro jumped to his feet. He tried not to look at Barbara.

"Yahhhhhhhhhhhhhh...!" Kuzaku instantly took down five or six of the spear squadron with a flash of his large katana.

There was a Hundred with a red spear in the squadron. Setora dodged its downward swing, stepped on the spear shaft, and snatched it away before bludgeoning the Hundred with its butt. Once the spear squadron's formation deteriorated, Anthony broke through.

"Dark!" Shihoru cried as she sent Dark careening into the squadron. Dark let out a *shooooooooooo* as he raced between the goblins, throwing them into disarray. Merry stuck close to Shihoru. Haruhiro was about to charge the squadron as well— but why were they the only ones doing this?

Barbara was Haruhiro's teacher. There was no way she'd let her guard down. They must have detected her while she was assessing the situation, then caught and killed her. In other words, the goblins they faced were skilled.

Had they underestimated their foes?

Goblins were smaller than humans. From a human perspective, they were ugly too. There was no way those creatures could be superior to humans. They weren't even equal. They had to be inferior. Could Haruhiro say he hadn't thought that?

He turned and was shocked. Behind either side of the black-cloaked soldiers led by Commander Dylan, a great number of goblins poured out of the shadows of the massive objects and swarmed toward them. Several carried red weapons. Commander Dylan and his men hadn't noticed at all and were just pushing forward. Commander Dylan—no, the whole raid team—was about to be taken by surprise. They'd been caught in a trap.

The spear squadron had been a decoy. Bait to lure out the raid team.

"Commander—"

Haruhiro didn't have time to get the man's name out. Before he could, a red-armored goblin lunged at Commander Dylan from behind and grabbed him by the hair with its left hand. In its right, it held something that was more of a knife than a dagger.

Commander Dylan didn't even resist. He had no time to. The red-armored goblin swiftly parted his head from his body in a fluid, wave-like motion that seemed well-practiced. That goblin had surely acquired several heads like that. Perhaps dozens. It might even have been the goblin that killed Barbara.

The red-armored goblin stomped on the stump of Commander Dylan's neck and swung the severed head around. "Ahh! Gyahh! Hahhhhhhhh...!"

Neal the scout had called Commander Dylan "the reaper himself." No matter how many of his men he let die, he always survived. He was a horrible man, but from his soldiers' perspective, there was a warped sense of trust, even relief in the fact that no matter what happened, the commander would be all right.

No one could remain standing after seeing their sole support cut down like that. Not a single black-cloaked soldier was still putting up a proper resistance. Three, maybe four of them were still breathing, but the goblins whaled on them.

Haruhiro felt enervated too. His eyes blurred, losing focus.

No, I can't give up before it's over, he tried to tell himself, but this wasn't a situation that could be overcome by appeals to willpower anymore. If you threw someone from a height of one hundred meters and told them to somehow survive, it would be impossible. You couldn't do what you couldn't do.

There were times when there was nothing you could do. You just had to accept it.

If Haruhiro were alone, he could have accepted it. The problem was, he had comrades. Even if he could write off his own death as inevitable, he didn't want to see his comrades end up like Barbara. Wasn't there anything to do?

That aside, he could see well. This was different from constantly swiveling his head, moving his eyeballs, and looking. It was as if he had left his own body. To say he was looking down from the sky would have been an exaggeration, but it was like he was seeing the area from an overhead angle.

He might not have been able to see the moves that the goblins, his team, or Anthony's men were making, but he could sense them. Each moved on their own in a chaotic mess, and he had a vague sense of all of them.

Haruhiro was submerged in the middle of it all. For whatever reason, at this moment, the goblins—even his comrades—were paying Haruhiro no heed. Haruhiro was unquestionably *here*, but it was as if he was nowhere at all.

On this bloody, violent, chaotic battlefield, Haruhiro was the one person with a presence as faint as a corpse. Thanks to that, no one noticed him.

Wasn't Barbara-sensei like this too? thought Haruhiro.

Maybe it was because they were in the forest at the time, but she had felt like a plant to him. No—because he hadn't been able to sense Barbara was there, Haruhiro had thought it was strange, and his mind had interpreted her as a plant.

Is this what it's like, Barbara-sensei? This is what Sensei was showing me then. I never expected it to be her last gift.

The red-armored goblin was obviously better outfitted than the others, and noticeably bigger too. That had to be Viceroy Bogg.

Bogg threw Commander Dylan's head into the air and let out a cry that went something like, "Gugai, gugai, gaigaih!" He sheathed his knife and drew the sword on his back. Its blade, as you would expect, was red.

The black-cloaked soldiers were all dead. The goblins led by Bogg rushed toward the rest of the raid team, who were still fighting the spear squadron.

Even when one or two of the goblins ran past Haruhiro, he didn't move. He slumped his shoulders, curved his back a little, and bent his knees slightly. No one noticed him. The important thing was his goal. He needed to set an appropriate goal.

Bogg ran straight toward him. At this rate, the goblin might run right into him. Even so, Haruhiro stayed put.

Kill Bogg. That's the goal.

When Bogg got to within about fifty centimeters of Haruhiro—so close he could have reached out and touched the goblin—only then did Bogg finally register that something was there. The viceroy came to a sudden stop, swinging his red sword with both hands.

Haruhiro stepped forward.

The red sword swung diagonally. Haruhiro leaned to the left as he advanced. He took a gash from the left side of his forehead to below his right eye, one that was not at all shallow, but he didn't care.

Haruhiro passed Bogg. As he did, the dagger he held in a backhand grip thrust out behind him. Maybe Bogg found some meaning in showing his face, because he wore no helmet.

Haruhiro's dagger did not stab into the back of Bogg's head. Bogg had twisted and dodged it at the last second. However, he hadn't been able to get out of the way completely. Haruhiro felt the blade gouge something hard. His dagger had carved a line in Bogg's skull. That was all. He hadn't taken the viceroy down.

He'd thought he could do it. But being frustrated wasn't going to help. Things happened. He had to react accordingly.

Haruhiro hadn't achieved his goal yet. There was more to come. He turned around.

Bogg's eyes widened and he glared at Haruhiro, holding the back of his head with his left hand. "Nggh, gahhhh...!"

He seemed enraged, but more than that, Bogg was confused. It felt to him like Haruhiro had appeared out of nowhere, right before his eyes, and nearly dealt him a fatal blow. It would be weirder if he weren't shocked by that.

The other goblins that had been about to attack the raid team were surprised too.

But Haruhiro was surrounded by Bogg's goblins, so if he messed this up, he was finished. He did feel some frustration and despair at the thought, *Why couldn't I have ended it with that one blow?* He was uneasy, and frightened. He had to suppress that and not lose the initiative.

"Kuzaaaaku! Anthonyyyy! Viceroy Bogg is over here!" As Haruhiro shouted, he drew his other dagger and swung at Bogg.

Bogg backed away, blocking Haruhiro's dagger with his sword. Haruhiro was dual wielding, and there wasn't much distance between them. In his confused state, the best Bogg could do was block a dagger with the crossguard of his sword. If they kept trading blows at such close range, the other goblins couldn't intervene.

Haruhiro didn't think he could push through. Naturally, he wanted to break through Bogg's defenses and end it all with this one-on-one duel, but a strong wish had a way of making people get too fixated, too tense, and rush things.

Besides, Bogg was stubborn. His body was tough, and he used his sword with skill. It was going to be hard to land a surprise fatal blow on him in a fair fight. The goal was to kill Bogg, but Haruhiro would have to take a number of steps to reach it.

Bogg deflected Haruhiro's dagger with the guard of his sword for more than the tenth time. It was his left-hand dagger, the flame one. In that moment, Haruhiro brought out the dagger in his right hand.

Bogg was holding his sword in both hands. Haruhiro's dagger gouged his left, severing the viceroy's fingers. Two of them, his little finger and ring finger, were gone completely.

Bogg cried, "Datts—!" or something close to that, and let go of his sword with his damaged hand. Now that he only held it in one hand, Bogg's power was guaranteed to be lower. Haruhiro was a step closer to his goal. He didn't intend to push there all in one go. Was that good or bad? He didn't know, but either way, Haruhiro couldn't predict what Bogg was going to do.

Bogg used his left hand, the one that had lost two fingers, to draw a knife and throw it.

Haruhiro twisted unconsciously. If he hadn't, Bogg's knife would have hit him right in the face. So he'd had no choice, but still, the goblin had gotten him. The moment Bogg had thrown his knife, he turned heel.

"Ngyagah...!"

And gave the order to retreat?

Bogg was running. It took him no time. He ran behind one of the tall objects and was out of sight.

Haruhiro ran after Bogg, not even wasting time to shout *You think you can escape?* Realizing his field of view had narrowed, he shook his head and glanced around. The goblins retreated without delay. He couldn't find Anthony and his men, but he could hear Kuzaku's battle cry. He was pretty close. Bogg was still nowhere to be seen, but Haruhiro had an idea of where he was going. It had to be Tenboro Tower.

Haruhiro soon spotted Bogg from behind. It was like he'd thought. Bogg was heading for Tenboro Tower. He apparently didn't plan on making any detours. He wouldn't take a round-about route either, obviously. This was the plaza in front of Tenboro Tower. When Bogg came out onto the road, the tower was already right in front of his nose.

The barricade they had erected in front of the main gate had an abatis—was that what those things were called? It was a line of sharpened pieces of lumber and metal pointing outward, bound together with string and wire, then reinforced with shields, iron plates, hides, and more. It looked like a confusing mess, but if manned properly, it would provide a considerable defensive advantage.

Bogg was about fifteen meters from the barricade, and Haruhiro was maybe eighteen. This roughly three-meter gap felt both large but small, and small but large.

Bogg glanced behind him—at Haruhiro, basically. He didn't seem surprised by how close Haruhiro was. It was like he was just verifying it, but simultaneously plotting something.

Haruhiro's goal was to kill Bogg. What was Bogg's? Was it to flee into Tenboro Tower?

It was something else, wasn't it?

"Haruhiro!" Kuzaku shouted from behind.

Even without turning around, Haruhiro could tell it wasn't just Kuzaku. Several of his comrades had come after him.

Bogg shouted, "Higyahhah!" Was that an order of some sort?

Multiple goblins stuck their faces out from the abatis. They'd been hiding. They held something in their hands.

Right in front of the abatis, Bogg lowered his posture, as if sliding across the cobblestones.

What the goblins on the abatis had in their hands were crossbows. There were more than ten of them.

"Get down!" Haruhiro said as he ducked himself.

The goblins on the abatis fired their bolts. Haruhiro stayed down, his head facing the rear. Kuzaku was there, taking point.

Setora, Kiichi, Merry, and Shihoru were there too, as well as Anthony and his men. They already knew the bolts were coming. Setora was crouching. Merry and Shihoru stood there, eyes wide.

"Ohh!" said Anthony.

It wasn't clear what Kuzaku was thinking, but he spread his arms wide with his large katana still gripped in his right hand. He spread his feet about as wide as his shoulders and puffed out his chest. It looked almost like he was trying to block the way—no, that was *exactly* what he was doing.

Kuzaku was trying to not let a single bolt pass, because his comrades were behind him. No matter how many bolts came flying, he was trying to block them all with his own body and protect his comrades.

I'm huge, you know? My body's just way too big, and that gets in the way sometimes, but it can also be useful at times like this, huh? That seemed like something Kuzaku might say with a laugh.

Man, that's the thing about you... Haruhiro thought. One after another, the bolts pierced Kuzaku's chest and belly. It seemed almost excessive. Five or six bolts—no, even more than that—easily penetrated Kuzaku's armor.

You're too damn cool sometimes.

Anthony took a bolt to the chest. "Gah!" he groaned and nearly doubled over before falling to one knee.

Kuzaku was still standing, but not fully upright, and unmoving. He coughed up blood once, then twice, and blinked. Not wanting to spew any more blood, he shut his lips tight, but each time he coughed, blood gushed out of his nose.

What now? thought Haruhiro. *What should I prioritize? I know I need to aim for the goal, but is that really important?*

"Kuzaku!"

"Kuzaku-kun!"

Setora and Shihoru shouted the name of their comrade. Merry rushed to his side.

Haruhiro jumped to his feet and turned back.

No. Kuzaku. Ahhh. No. No, that's not okay. It's not. I'm sorry, Barbara-sensei, I can't do this anymore. Kuzaku. Kuzaku can't stand much longer. Those aren't wounds you can stand with. It's impossible. It's crazy.

Kuzaku fell backward. Merry caught him, but he was heavy. It looked like she was going to fall over. Haruhiro had to make it there and help Merry support Kuzaku.

"Again!" Setora warned sharply.

Haruhiro looked at the abatis. The goblins were looking out from it. Bogg was on the other side. He'd climbed onto some sort of platform and was taking command.

The goblins on the abatis took aim with their crossbows. Had they already reloaded? Or maybe they'd had extra crossbows loaded in advance.

"Merry!" Haruhiro called out as he hurriedly carried Kuzaku to the side of the street. In the midst of the flying bolts, they dragged Kuzaku into the shadow of one of the massive objects.

"Haruhiro," Kuzaku gasped.

Kuzaku was limp. He'd dropped his large katana at some point, because he wasn't holding it now. There were three bolts in Kuzaku's chest, another in his right shoulder, one in his left arm, and two more buried deep in his stomach. He opened and closed his eyes, perhaps desperately trying to hold on to his fading consciousness. In a weak voice, he repeated, "Haruhiro."

"Wh-what? What is it, Kuzaku?" Haruhiro brought his face closer to Kuzaku's. *Huh? What's this?* he thought. *I feel like I remember.*

Kuzaku gripped Haruhiro's left arm in his right hand with surprising strength. "I'm... so...rry..."

"Huh? What? S-sorry? Why? What...?" *I feel like this has happened before.*

Kuzaku's pallor was awful. Drained of blood; not white, or blue, but ashen.

Not with Kuzaku. Someone else.

"Manato," Haruhiro whispered.

That's right. Kuzaku's going to die like Manato... That can't happen.

"You can't, Kuzaku!"

"I'm...so—"

Is that why Kuzaku's apologizing? "Looks like I'm going to die, sorry for dying," is that it? "Don't be stupid!"

"Move!" Merry pulled Haruhiro away from him. She pressed her right hand to Kuzaku. Then, using her left hand to check the bolts sticking out of his body, she decided. "He can still make it! Pull those bolts out! As fast as you can! All of them! There's no point healing him with magic while they're still there! Haru! Setora! Shihoru, you help too!"

Up until that point, Haruhiro hadn't noticed that Setora, Shihoru, and Kiichi were right beside them. What were Anthony and his men doing? That crossed his mind for a second, but Kuzaku came first.

Merry said he was going to make it. Right. Merry could heal Kuzaku with magic. But the wounds couldn't close with bolts inside them. There was going to be massive bleeding when they pulled them out, and that was dangerous, but they'd do it. Pull all the bolts out at once, then, without missing a beat, Merry would use her magic. They had to do it.

There were seven bolts. They needed Merry to prepare her magic. Haruhiro would do two, Setora would do two, Shihoru would do two, and Kiichi would do the last one. They'd need Kiichi to help too. Kuzaku was already unresponsive, his closed eyes twitching. It wasn't clear how much longer he'd last, and there wasn't time. There was no other way. But could the nyaa do it?

"It's okay!" Setora was on the job.

Merry pressed her fingers to her forehead, and the rest of the group gripped their respective bolts. She began chanting a prayer. "O Light, may Lumiaris's divine protection be upon you."

"Ready, go!" Haruhiro shouted.

Haruhiro, Setora, Shihoru, and Kiichi all pulled the bolts out of Kuzaku in unison.

Merry turned both hands toward Kuzaku. "Sacrament!"

Looking at that intense light, Haruhiro was temporarily blinded.

"Aw, yeah!" he heard Kuzaku say.

This is not an "Aw, yeah!" situation, thought Haruhiro as he rubbed his eyes.

Kuzaku was already standing up. "I live again! Thanks, everyone!"

"You live again?" Merry sounded exasperated. "*You* never even died."

"Let's not sweat the small stuff!" Kuzaku said with a smile.

Haruhiro rubbed his eyes again. "Man, you are such a..."

"Huh, Haruhiro, are you crying?" Kuzaku said something he really shouldn't have.

"I am not!" Haruhiro said back, sticking his face out from behind the massive object and looking toward the abatis. Bogg was up on his platform, waving his red sword around and screeching wildly. The goblins on the abatis seemed to be working on something. Probably loading crossbows.

Anthony was taking shelter behind the massive object directly across the street from them. He was alone. Two of his men were collapsed in the street. Anthony himself had a bolt in his right breast and probably couldn't move properly. Having Merry heal Anthony with magic was sadly going to have to wait.

"Kuzaku, charge straight in! Everyone, back him up!"

"On it!" Kuzaku said, energetically licking his lips. "When you know that anything that doesn't kill you can instantly be fixed, it's crazy how brave you can be!"

"You idiot!" Setora whacked Kuzaku on the back of the head. "I won't tolerate you getting yourself half-killed again!"

"It's not good for my heart!" Shihoru said in a rare accusatory tone.

"Heh," Kuzaku bashfully bowed his head. "Sorry."

"I won't let you cross that final line!" Merry said firmly, then looked to Haruhiro. That dignified smile... He remembered it. There were times when Merry was just too beautiful, crossing into otherworldly.

"We're counting on you!" was all Haruhiro said before rushing out.

He didn't need to watch. Kuzaku would jump out into the road, pick up his large katana, and charge the abatis. His comrades would follow Kuzaku. Shihoru would launch Dark, Merry would protect Shihoru, and Setora and Kiichi would support Kuzaku.

Haruhiro ran off on his own, threading between the massive objects, and headed toward Tenboro Tower.

"Haaahhhh! Bring it!" Kuzaku was in the street, provoking the enemy.

It seemed the goblins on the abatis hadn't finished reloading their crossbows yet. If they had, they'd long since have fired them.

Kuzaku and the others would play their part well. They'd draw the enemy's attention. Haruhiro approached the abatis in front of Tenboro Tower from the side.

Submerge. Submerge it. My own presence. My very existence. No, don't submerge. Sink. Just sink in smoothly.

Bogg kicked another goblin off the platform. He insulted and rushed his troops, like he was saying, "Hurry up, you slow idiots!"

The goblins on the abatis gave up on reloading their crossbows and cast them aside, picking up long spears instead. They thrust the spears through the abatis, likely trying to keep Kuzaku in check. As if to show them it was futile, Kuzaku swung his large katana and cut apart a number of the spears. "Kyahhh! Hah!" he cried.

Bogg gave up on the goblins manning the abatis and jumped down from the platform, rushing inside Tenboro Tower through the doorless main gate.

He never even suspected that Haruhiro had crept up right behind him.

Haruhiro silently climbed over the abatis and grappled Bogg from behind. That was the first moment that Bogg registered his existence. Haruhiro slit Bogg's throat with his dagger. When he was this close, he couldn't possibly screw it up. Bogg may have wanted to hurl some hateful invective at him as he died, but his windpipe was torn open. The goblin wasn't going to be saying anything.

Haruhiro pushed Bogg to the ground, seizing the goblin's head with his left hand. Haruhiro then used the dagger in his right hand to quickly sever everything but the goblin's spine, which he twisted and broke with brute force.

If he said he wasn't emotional, he'd be lying, but he did his best to keep his feelings under control. The truth was, he wanted to carve Bogg's corpse up right now, kick it around, and reduce it to mincemeat. But Barbara would probably have laughed at him, saying, *"Now, listen. What good is that going to do, Old Cat? That's not what you should be doing, right?"*

Haruhiro didn't get riled easily. Barbara-sensei had told him he wasn't the type that could do things if he tried, he was the type that tried until he could do them. If that was true—and he had no doubt it was—as her humble student, that was how he wanted to be.

If he could become a thief who never missed a trick, always living on his own terms, like an old cat, then maybe that would let him repay her in some small way.

Haruhiro stood, Bogg's severed head in his left hand. *We've won,* he thought, but he didn't say it out loud. For someone like him, with the sleepy eyes of an old cat, those words didn't seem right.

Grimgar *of* *Fantasy* *and* *Ash*

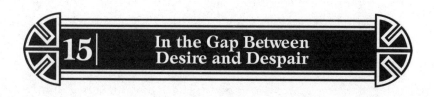

15 | In the Gap Between Desire and Despair

WHEN THEY LEARNED of the death of Viceroy Bogg, the goblins of Alterna instantly lost the will to fight. The suicide squad, who had somehow not been completely annihilated, opened the south gate, and the main body of the Expeditionary Force flooded into Alterna. Meanwhile, Haruhiro's group opened the north gate, as per General Jin Mogis's strategy.

Everything went as planned. The main force caught the goblins as they were massed at the north gate, trying to get out, and massacred a great number of them. In the meantime, Haruhiro's group carried the bodies of Barbara, Anthony Justeen's subordinates, and even Dylan Stone and his men into Tenboro Tower. The battle had long since been decided. General Mogis ordered one of his close associates to carry out a cleanup operation and went to Tenboro Tower.

There had been female goblins in Tenboro Tower, but they had already either fled or been killed in the process. Before the humans set foot inside, it was clear that there wasn't a person—no, a goblin—to be found in the whole place.

When General Mogis saw the bodies lined up in the entrance hall, including Commander Dylan, he made the sign of the hexagram with his fingers, then smiled a little.

"Is something funny?" Anthony asked, his voice shaking.

To be honest, Haruhiro wanted to ask the general the same thing, so he was grateful Anthony did it for him, though he didn't expect a proper answer to be forthcoming. It wasn't.

The general put a hand on Anthony's shoulder. "I'll need to do an inspection of the castle. Come with me."

It was as if those rusty eyes of his were fake, and he saw nothing with them. Just how heartless was this man? He was harder to read than the goblins, and they were a completely different race. This was why Barbara-sensei had been suspicious and distrustful of the general.

Haruhiro's group and Anthony followed the general as he toured the first floor where the entrance hall and the storage were located, then the second floor, which contained the great hall, the audience chamber, the kitchens, and more. There was no sign of damage, so perhaps Viceroy Bogg and those under him had lived a vaguely human-like lifestyle here.

When they ascended the spiral staircase to the third floor, they heard a faint voice. "Heyyyy... Heyyyy... Anyoooone... Is anyone theeere...? Heeeelp meeee..."

The voice was clearly human.

Unlike the first and second floors, which were exactly what

you might expect from a lord's keep, the building was essentially a tower from the third floor up. The stairs and hallways ate up more than half the floor space on each level, and there were only three or four rooms, none of which were especially big. Some doors were closed, but others were open.

Finding nothing unusual on the third floor, they moved up to the fourth.

"Heyyyy. Heyyyy. Is anyone there? I'm in heeeere. Come heeeelp. Heyyyy..."

Haruhiro walked into a room on the fourth floor. The door was wide open. "Oh."

This had probably been the bedroom of a person of high status. But the marvelous bed had been lifted up and leaned against the wall, replaced, if you could call it that, with an iron cage that now dominated the center of the room. The person inside it was probably a human man. He was naked, so that wasn't really in question.

"Wh-who are you?! No, it doesn't matter! Save me!" the naked man shouted, pressing his nose up against the bars. "I am the Lord of Alterna, the representative of the Kingdom of Arabakia in the frontier! You must know the name of Margrave Garlan Vedoy! Now, hurry and let me out of here!"

The man was emaciated, his hair and beard overgrown, and his entire body covered with grime. His eyes were bloodshot, and he made no attempt to hide his genitals. There was a pot in the corner, probably meant for him to use as a toilet. Though it had a lid on it, there was a beastly stench in the air. It didn't matter who he was; he seemed pitiful, and Haruhiro wanted to let him out. That said, it was also a fact that he was off-putting. Haruhiro wasn't the only one to feel that way.

"Whoa..." Kuzaku said when he entered the room, and he backed away.

"Ugh!" Setora, who had Kiichi on her shoulders, gulped, and Merry and Shihoru both yelped.

Anthony, who might have once been in a position to serve the Margrave, said, "This is..." before falling silent, unable to say any more.

Finally, General Mogis shoved Haruhiro aside and stepped forward.

"Ohh!" The Margrave's eyes widened. "That cape! Are you one of the Black Hounds, from the mainland?!"

"I am Jin Mogis, Margrave," the general introduced himself, putting his hand on the hilt of his sword.

"I see! Jin Mogis, is it? I don't know you, but let me out! That's an order!"

"This is a sad state to be in for the man who is supposed to represent the Kingdom of Arabakia in the frontier."

"S-silence! You dare mock me?! I am Garlan Vedoy!"

"I am aware. The House of Vedoy has been famous ever since George I, also known as Theodore George, established the Kingdom of Arabakia."

"I can see you're different from the ignorant trash of the frontier! Someone from the mainland like you can see that not only am I a noble, I also bear noble blood!"

"You are noble, yes, but also incompetent."

"Wha—"

"Defeated by another race, you languished in prison, naked and dripping feces. I am aghast that you survived this long without taking your own life."

"Do you think I feel no shame in this?!"

"If you feel ashamed, then die at once."

"Th-that's absurd."

"Give up. You should thank me for this."

"Thank you?"

"I am saying I will defend your honor."

General Mogis drew his sword. The caged Margrave didn't run. He might have simply never imagined this could happen. Haruhiro had half-predicted it, but he couldn't stop it.

The general ran the Margrave through. "You were long dead."

"Long..." The Margrave looked down at the sword in his chest, then back to the general and tried to repeat the words again. "Long... dead..."

"The way I see it," the general spoke plainly. "The proud Margrave, unable to submit to imprisonment by the lesser races, ended his own life."

"I-I..."

"This is better than living in shame. I have saved you, Garlan Vedoy."

The Margrave was still trying to say something. However, when the general pulled his sword out, he collapsed against the bars of his cage. He was quivering, so he wasn't dead yet, but it was only a matter of time.

When Merry rushed forward, the general turned toward them, bloody sword still in hand. "Do you wish to offer a prayer for the Margrave, priest of Lumiaris? If so, there's no need to hurry. He's not dead yet."

Obviously, Merry had intended to heal the Margrave. Haruhiro had no grudge against the man, and there were things he'd wanted to ask him about. Maybe they should save the Margrave, even if it meant taking out the general to do it.

"Merry," was all Haruhiro said, then shook his head.

Merry nodded and backed down. There was nothing they could do. While Haruhiro struggled with his decision, the Margrave took his last breath and moved no more. The general must have pierced his heart. Judging from how fast he bled out, there would have been no saving him either way.

The general wiped the blood from the sword onto his black fur cloak, and then returned it to its scabbard. "Anthony."

"Yes, sir!" Anthony replied, looking down.

"I've heard that the Margrave was also called the king of the frontier," said the general.

"Certainly..." Anthony strained to get the words out, "there were some who called him that..."

"Regrettably, the Margrave is no more," the general said, glancing at the cage. "I will rule Alterna in his place for the time being, as king of the frontier."

Sensei, Haruhiro spoke to Barbara in his heart. *General Mogis really is bad news. If we let him have his way, no good will come of it.*

I wish I could have learned more from you, so I could stop him. I wish I could have borrowed your strength. But this sleepy-eyed Old Cat will shed no tears. It's all just begun. It's too soon for despair.

Grimgar of Fantasy and Ash

16 | Another

AROUND THE SAME TIME, there might have been a masked man, a fierce tempest of swords, leaving a fine red mist and a torrent of screams wherever he passed as he continued, still, to slash.

Or perhaps there wasn't.

No. The masked man existed. He existed, all right?

Riverside Iron Fortress—that hardened fortress along the Jet River that was now a kobold den—was subjected to a violent assault before dawn. The unrelenting torrent of Blasts, Detonations, and even high level Arve Magic like Blaze Falls, as well as Thunderbolts, Thunderstorms, and Icicle Downs was highly effective. The kobolds' earnest attempts to defend the fortress were meaningless before the storm, and they were broken in no time.

But the battle was just getting started.

The kobolds had an especially strong pack instinct. When led by one of the high-ranking kobolds who lived in the depths of the Cyrene Mines, the countless worker kobolds—and even the elder kobolds who oversaw them—would fight without fear of death. Within moments, the fortress interior was utter pandemonium. The kobolds piled up their own corpses to defend their positions. While the attackers busily removed the corpses, more kobold reinforcements arrived to initiate a pincer attack.

But the masked man had known this would be a fight to the death, and unlike those useless grunts in the Frontier Army, from the day he had become a volunteer soldier, he had risked his life to keep himself fed, and gained fame by relying only on himself and his comrades.

Any battle where you could maintain your composure didn't even count as a battle at all. Anyone who hadn't thought, *Aw, crap, I'm dead, this is the end,* at least a hundred times was just a scrub.

What did he have to hide? No, he had no intention of hiding it. Sink-or-swim, life-or-death, kill-or-be-killed situations were daily hurdles for volunteer soldiers.

In order to survive, the volunteer soldiers inside the fortress killed kobolds like crazy, then were nearly killed by kobolds in return. They ignored the wounds that didn't keep them from moving and had priests use light magic to heal the really debilitating ones. Then they went back to killing and almost being killed by kobolds again. If that was your daily life, you would get sick of it. It would be unbearable. But even when they were put in a situation that should have made them say *"No, no, no, I can't take this anymore, I just want to die. Let it end already. Somebody, kill me, please! Somebody!"* the volunteer soldiers didn't let it get them down.

Well, no, not all of the volunteer soldiers were actually that tough. But most of the volunteer soldiers who were participating in the attack on Riverside Iron Fortress today were real badasses, and they had seen their share of battles.

It went without saying that the masked man was one of them.

There were a total of fourteen towers that made up Riverside Iron Fortress, connected by bridges so that they could move forces from one to another. Because of that, it was theoretically possible to keep up a defensive line until all fourteen towers fell. They had to take the towers one by one until either the attackers' or the defenders' will to fight gave out.

The masked man was heading for the top floor of the seventh tower. If this were a mountain, he'd already be at the seventh station. No, maybe it would be the fifth, or the eighth, or even the ninth. The stairs were less than two meters wide, and they were packed tight with lines of kobolds, thrusting weapons like spears and naginatas at him. It would be suicide to charge straight into that. That's what anyone would think. But just throwing himself at it anyway was the masked man's style, his philosophy, his way of life.

"Personal skill!"

The masked man took a swing with his katana and rushed up the stairs. The kobolds all barked and tried to skewer him or cut him up with their polearms. If he just charged in like a raging bull, even if he was the toughest of the tough guys, that was exactly what would happen to him.

"Holy Lightning Brahma-Deva Sovereign Strike!"

So, before the kobolds could skewer him, the masked man jumped. He leapt to the left and kicked off the wall, springing back to the right. The kobolds let out confused barks as they swung their polearms. They reflexively tried to follow the masked man.

It was no use. The masked man moved with lightning reflexes. There was no way they could keep up. He kicked off the left wall, then the right, then the left again, before finally landing in the middle of the kobolds. He slashed and slashed and slashed some more. The masked man had been soaked with kobold blood to begin with, but now it was even worse, and he didn't stop slicing and dicing as he whittled their numbers down. Every muscle in his body cried out in protest, and his lungs felt like they were ready to burst, but the masked man would not stop. For he was a fiend, a devil, a demon.

Whatever he was, whatever he wished to be, the masked man was not God, not one of God's children, and not even a monster. Once his katana had tasted the blood of fifteen, no, seventeen or eighteen kobolds, the masked man suddenly felt exhausted. *Oh, crap! What is this? My body won't do what I tell it. I can't even talk. I'm running out of stamina here? Seriously? I mean, seriously?*

The kobolds howled like they were going *Now, now's our chance, get 'im!* They stepped over the slashed-up corpses of their comrades, or kicked them out of the way, and swarmed toward the masked man. The man raised his head. He was aware of them, but there was nothing he could do.

The hell? What's a guy as awesome as me doing, screwing up like this here? Damn it.

"Stupid Ranta!"

Then a hunter with her long hair tied in braids jumped out, firing an arrow toward the kobolds. She was carrying a bow. A short bow. She nocked another arrow and loosed it. Incredibly fast. And every shot she took hit a kobold in the eye or the mouth. Even at close range like this, no, especially at close range like this, because of the pressure her targets put on her, it was hard to pull off shots like that. The hunter had just done something incredibly difficult, and she did it easily, as if it were no trouble at all.

Just how many kobolds had she killed by the time her quiver was empty? Seven or eight, at least. "You're a real armful, y'know that?!" Using an expression that was only partly right, she grabbed the masked man by the scruff of his neck and dragged him down the stairs before the kobolds could reach them.

"Hey, that hurts! You're choking me, Yume! Damn it!"

"It's your fault for bein' reckless, stupid Ranta! Suffer more!"

"I'm suffering plenty already!"

"Everyone!" Yume gave the signal.

Volunteer soldiers kept running past the masked man—who some knew as Ranta—and Yume, but it was a narrow corridor. In no time, they were pressed against the wall together.

"Whoa?!"

"Meow?!"

Yume had the wall to her back and Ranta was covering her.

He wasn't on top of her or anything, but if he didn't do this, it would be a little dangerous or something, y'know?

"G-guys...!" Ranta protested, but no one was listening. The other volunteer soldiers were stepping into the gap that Ranta and, well, Yume had opened, and were trying to crush the enemy with one more push. They were all going to town on the kobolds.

"Y-Yume! Let me just say, this wasn't intentional, okay?!"

"What wasn't?!"

"What wasn't? Now, listen..." There were times when Ranta was really glad he wore a mask. Their bodies were pressed together as much as they possibly could be, so naturally, their faces were close, and it was kind of, uh, embarrassing.

It wasn't bad, but still. He felt like it had perked him up a little, so maybe it wasn't just not bad, it was good? Because Ranta still had to swing his katana.

The battle wasn't over yet.

VOLUME 15 CAME QUICKLY. No, maybe not quickly at all. For me, it feels like it's been a very long time, and I wrote the first volume a long, long time ago.

This is Volume 15, but it's not the fifteenth volume to come out. The preceding volumes, compiled in Volume 14.5, have stories about Ranta and Yume. Those might look like side stories based on the volume numbering, but the content isn't really side material, so if you haven't read them, I believe doing so will help you enjoy the series more.

Now we've entered the Endgame Chapter. Well, that's just what I'm calling it myself, but it is, literally, the endgame. However, we haven't decided on the exact number of volumes remaining, so I hope Haruhiro and the others' journey can continue as long as possible. Please, continue to support me.

Now then, to my editor, Harada-san, to the illustrator, Eiri Shirai-san, to the designers of KOMEWORKS, among others, to everyone involved in production and sale of this book, and finally to all of you people now holding this book: I offer my heartfelt appreciation and all of my love. Now, I lay down my pen for today.

I hope we will meet again.

—Ao Jyumonji

Grimgar of Fantasy and Ash

Let your imagination take flight with Seven Seas' light novel imprint: Airship

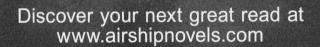

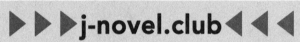